STRANDED WITH HER RESCUER

BY

NIKKI LOGAN

MILLS & BOON

First published in Great Britain 2016
By Mills & Boon, an imprint of HarperCollins*Publishers*
1 London Bridge Street, London, SE1 9GF

Large Print edition 2016

© 2016 Nikki Logan

ISBN: 978-0-263-26248-3

For my beautiful boy, Gus.
The sonorous metronome
to which I wrote my books.
How you would have loved all this snow.

'Dogs are wise.
They crawl into a quiet corner
and lick their wounds and do not re-join
the world until they are whole once more.'
—Agatha Christie

Acknowledgements

A huge shout-out to Bill, Rita and Bos from
Up the Creek, who looked after me like
I was family back in October 2014 when I
was researching this book in the sub-arctic.
And to the teachers of Thompson, Manitoba,
who shared with me an unforgettable day on
the tundra during which I saw my first wild
polar bear and my first wild snow—
though sadly not at the same time.

PROLOGUE

Five years ago, Pokhara, Nepal.

WILL MARGRAVE LEANED a shoulder against the rounded earthen interior wall of his villa overlooking Pokhara and peered through the window down to the terrace flats below. The topmost flat was furred with the gentle, swaying grasses native to this part of Nepal, peppered with small clusters of shrubs and fully fenced all the way around to the kennels out back of the house. The yard had to be large, to do its job housing his sixteen rescue dogs.

Maybe it was the richness of the light, or the majesty of the mountains or the mirrored reflection of Phewa Lake but everything in this environment just sat so...comfortably in it.

Including him.

Will leaned forward into the window's curve to watch the solitary woman below mingling with his dogs. Kitty Callaghan liked to start her day early and she liked to start it outside. On her second day here, he'd spotted her halfway down the terraces, meditating under the watchful protection of the Annapurnas as the sun rose behind the mountain range, doing her best impersonation of a normal, still person. Usually she was anything but, and today she was clearly in a more active mood, jogging back and forth in the fenced-in yard, tapping the noses of one dog then the next and darting back out of reach as they joined the game, drawing a canine cluster back and forth with her as she ran, not minding how silly she might look or how much dirt they kicked up.

Dogs and dirt didn't bother Kitty any more than the looming mountains and composting toilets did. It was one of the things he liked about her best.

Not everybody loved the silent granite sentinels that marked Nepal's border. Mountains were dominant, powerful forces—for better or worse. Some people found them oppressive and ominous, almost claustrophobic. People like his wife. Though how Marcella could stand anywhere on this hillside under these vast, wild skies and feel closed in was a mystery to him.

Like so much about her.

That mystery had once intrigued him—back

when he'd assumed her secrets would unfurl like a lotus as the months and years passed—but intrigue had a way of losing its appeal when your marriage eroded as steadily as the rock beneath your feet.

Down below, Kitty laughed as one dog got the better of her. She arched back when Quest reared up and placed his paws on her slight shoulders, her face turned up to the gentle morning light— twisted away from Quest's errant tongue—and the magic of her laughter cascaded like water down the terraced hillside.

And like warm breath down his spine.

Ugh… Moments like this one didn't help his resolve. Looking at those wide grey eyes in perfect pale skin and not wanting to just…dive right in to see what curiosities lay behind them. Sitting up late at night by the fire, hovering on the precipice of the kind of conversations he missed so desperately, lying to himself that he could get a handle on the feelings that had been escalating ever since she arrived ten short days ago to film her series of freelance pieces in Nepal.

Ten *long* days knowing that Marcella was the kind of woman he'd always wanted—glamorous, talented, creative—but beginning to fear that Kitty was the kind he actually *needed*.

And he didn't want to need anything from anyone who wasn't his wife.

Eleven months ago he'd given Marcella his promise along with his heart, and he was not about to betray either of those. If he had to break his word to a woman, it wasn't going to be the one he had pledged himself to in front of God.

They could make this marriage work—*he* could make it work.

Will shoved the ache down deep inside as he withdrew from the window. Kitty Callaghan needed to go. She didn't have to leave Nepal— she could finish up her work—she just had to get out of this house. This town.

This marriage.

And she needed to do it soon, before the questions her presence raised began to eat away at the foundations of his already shaky relationship.

Will balled his fingers into fists and headed for the stairs.

He wasn't even halfway down before his heart started hardening against her.

The slow rise of her head, the easy, surprised-to-see-you smile she offered him… It was all fake. Kitty knew the precise moment Will stepped out of his house, even as she had her back to him and the massive Annapurnas towering up behind him. She didn't need Quest's excited stare to tell her he was approaching, either.

She could feel him.

She could always feel him; in the tickle of her neck hairs and the tightening of her belly. Some kind of primitive intuition doing its thing. Still, she gave him her brightest, most welcoming smile. Because it was something she could do. A gesture that celebrated the bond she'd formed with him, in a perfectly appropriate way. One that said she knew exactly how lucky she was to be here.

'Morning, Will.'

'Got a moment, Kitty?'

There was something in the hard shadow in his eyes, the stiff way he was holding himself. The same way he did when one of his dogs indicated positive on a shard of clothing during a missing-hiker search. His tension infected her, too, and Quest fell away from their game, disappointed but accepting.

'Sure.'

Will held a courteous hand low to her back as he guided her out of the dog yard, then seemed to think better of it and tucked it down behind his own body. As if she were tainted.

'Something wrong? Is Marcella okay?'

Because some mornings his wife really wasn't. Those mornings she looked as if she hadn't slept more than an hour. If at all. And not in a good, first-year-of-marriage, up-all-night kind of way.

'Marcella's fine. I just need to speak to you.'

Instinct told her to get ahead of this conversation, to get some control over it. She spun to face him and he nearly barrelled into her. He caught himself just before impact, then stepped back as though—again—she were infected with something nasty. He backed up a little further for good measure.

That extra step particularly hurt.

'Something you didn't want the dogs to hear?' she joked, though it cost her.

'Kitty, I...' He glanced out at the mountains all around them for inspiration. This wasn't like him. The two of them had had nothing but easy conversations in the ten days she'd been in Nepal. Easy, deep, fabulous talks that felt as if they were continuing old exchanges from years ago.

'You're making me nervous, Will. What's going on?'

'I need to ask you to leave,' he blurted.

How embarrassing that her first response was to misunderstand him. She frowned and glanced back at the dogs. 'The yard? I thought it would be okay to—'

'Pokhara, Kitty. It's time for you to go.'

She blinked at him. 'No, it's not. I have nearly three weeks before it's time.'

And, boy, she was not looking forward to that day.

'Marcella shouldn't have invited you to stay the whole month. It's…' He gazed back at the mountains. 'It's too much, Kitty. Too long.'

An awful kind of humiliation washed through her. That she had presumed he would be okay with it just because his wife was. Or seemed to be.

'You said I was welcome,' she breathed.

In his own words, with no one twisting his arm.

'That's what you do say, in this situation, isn't it?'

When someone makes a horrendous presumption, did he mean?

'So…' Her head spun, and not just from the altitude. 'Was I never welcome or am I no longer welcome?'

She didn't really want to know the answer, either way, but she *absolutely* wanted to hear it from his lips.

'You've finished filming our rescue operation...'

Part of the heat that rushed up her throat was because, to an extent, Will was right. She'd finished the main filming for the dogs, she'd been enjoying Pokhara and getting a feel for the country since then. Imagining what a fantastic piece it was going to make, visually.

And spinning out her time with him.

'And we've got too much going on—'

'No, you don't.'

Marcella barely painted, never went out if she could avoid it; she lurked around their property alternating between long bouts of flat melancholy and excited bursts of energy. Meanwhile, Will trained every day but he had a comfortable routine that didn't wear the dogs out. And only two emergency calls in the ten days she'd been here.

His lips thinned as he stared at her. The first time he'd made actual eye contact.

'Kitty—'

'I pick up after myself. I went to the market on Monday to save Marcella the trouble.' And— PS—paid for a carload of supplies. 'So what's the real issue?'

Of course, a dignified person wouldn't ask. A dignified person would just accept that things had changed and head off to start packing. Smiling, thanking them and giving her hosts a modest gift when she went. But there was nothing dignified about the panic that Kitty was starting to feel at Will's decree, and not just because of the humiliation. Sometime between arriving and now, she'd realised that she was the happiest she'd ever been in Pokhara. Having that taken away was terrifying.

And the thought of never seeing Will again only compounded it.

'You can't really want to stay,' he urged. 'Knowing we don't want you here.'

Something told her that 'we' was actually 'I', because his wife had clung to her since the day she'd arrived, and Marcella was too Southern and too well brought up to renege on a promise.

'No,' she snorted. 'I don't. But I'm not leaving without knowing what I did to get myself banished.'

She had a sneaking suspicion, actually, and a whole new flood of shame went on standby, ready for his answer.

For the first time, he softened, and it was so

much worse than the hardened exterior he'd presented up until now. Because it was *Will*, not this icy doppelgänger.

'You must know, Kit. You're doing it right now.'

She lost her grip on the humiliation and it flooded her face. For ten days she'd worked so hard to keep a lid on her inappropriate feelings. To pretend the emotions didn't exist. But they had a habit of leaking out when she was with him. Any time she wasn't totally vigilant. Talking, laughing.

Or just standing very close, like this… Peering up at him.

'I…'

Really, what could she say? She knew she was feeling it, and she knew what she was feeling. She would be naïve to imagine she wasn't showing that at all, but Will hadn't let on before, or objected to the conversations, the shared space, the accidental body contact passing on the stairs.

She'd even begun to think he might have enjoyed it. Just a little bit.

Obviously not.

'It's okay, Kitty, I get it. We've been spending a lot of time together—'

Her heart hammered.

She wasn't about to be condescended to like a

teenager. If he'd picked up on her feelings, why had he indulged them? Why not just shut them right down?

Shame ached through her whole body.

This *was* him shutting them down.

'I just think it would be better for everyone if you headed off to do your own thing,' he said.

Get the heck off his mountain, he meant.

'We were friends,' she said, numb and flat. Too hurt and too confused to even put any energy behind the accusation.

His eyes darkened and swung away from her. 'You must want to see the rest of Nepal.'

No, not really. She'd been happy here, happier than any other time in her life. It was *this* mountain she loved, not just any Nepalese mountain. *This* town. *This* man.

That was why she had to go.

She could not love Will Margrave, and he certainly couldn't love her, even if he wanted to, which—judging by the enormous tension in his body—he did not.

'I'm married, Kitty.'

Yes, to the woman who'd invited her into their home. Was this how she'd repaid Marcella's kindness? By making her husband uncomfortable enough to ask her to leave?

She dropped her eyes to the dark, rich earth. She'd caused this. She had to be the one to fix it.

'Okay,' she murmured. 'I'll go.'

She stumbled away from Will without raising her eyes again. And she didn't look at him as she wrestled her stuffed backpack down the stairs, or as she hugged a weeping Marcella, or as she closed the door of the aging taxi behind her.

In fact, she didn't raise her gaze until she was safely away from that Pokhara hillside, just in case he saw something there she would never recover from. Something worse than love.

Shame.

Which made that pitying gaze out by the dogs' yard the last of Will Margrave she would ever see. And pity the last thing he would ever feel for her.

And she promised herself, in that moment, never to drop her eyes again.

CHAPTER ONE

Present day, Churchill, Canada.

'YOU MUST BE KIDDING!'

Kitty Callaghan bundled herself tighter in her complimentary blanket and swapped her hand luggage into her right hand to give her left a break.

'Sorry, ma'am,' the polite woman said, widening her arms to usher her towards the exit. 'Canadian federal law. No one can stay inside the airport after shutdown.'

'But I have nowhere to go,' she pointed out, though it was hardly necessary since this was the same official who'd been working for hours to find beds—or even sofas—for the one hundred and sixty-four passengers who'd found themselves stranded in their remote dot-on-a-map after smoke started billowing from their aircraft's cargo hold thirty-five thousand feet over Greenland.

'We've done everything we can to find accommodation for the final six of you. Three will be bunking down in the medical centre and two will be guests of the Mounties tonight in their holding cells. That's every bed we have in town.'

Which left her sitting up all night in some waiting room.

This was the price she paid for being good at her job. Or maybe for simply doing it. Airlines had a way of not appreciating it when you captured their stuff-ups for posterity. She'd been way too busy filming the whole emergency response that had followed the pilot's spectacular touchdown of the massive airliner on the remote, ice-patched runway to get herself higher up the queue for overnight accommodation. By the time she'd started paying attention to where she was going to spend the rest of the night, there had been no more room at the inn.

'You don't have a hotel here? Or even a B & B?'

The woman's compassion wasn't making her feel any better. 'Actually we have nearly as many hotel rooms as residents but they're all booked up because of bear season. And we're out of volunteers with sofas.'

'*Bear* season?' Kitty blinked her confusion, glancing around. 'Where are we exactly?'

Other than someplace snowy somewhere on a

high arc between Zurich and Los Angeles up over the top of the planet. She'd been sleeping comfortably when the captain had made his emergency announcement and the chaos that had followed really hadn't been the time to be pumping the flight crew with questions.

'Churchill, Manitoba, ma'am,' the woman said proudly. 'Polar bear capital of the world.'

Churchill...

All the ice the A340 had come sliding in on suddenly seemed to relocate to her chest.

She'd heard of Churchill...

'And what is bear season exactly?' she said, tightly, to buy herself the time she needed to get her fibrillating heart under control.

The woman smiled, oblivious to the sudden extra tension in the near-empty terminal. 'Oh, hundreds of bears migrate here to wait for Hudson Bay to freeze over, to go hunt on the ice for the winter. Numbers are at their peak right now. They're everywhere.'

'Maybe I could snuggle in between two of *them* for the night.'

The woman had a right to be disappointed at Kitty's tone, but *she* had a right to be snitchy. Her plane had caught fire in mid-air. She'd endured an emergency landing then been bounced out into the bitter cold via the emergency slides with nothing but the light dress on her back, the complimentary blanket she'd been snuggled in, and her cabin bag, which she'd packed with the minimalist precision of a pro. Just her camera gear, some basic toiletries and an e-reader; none of which were going to help her out here. She had nowhere to go for the night except the heated police station waiting room because apparently this one was off-limits. And to top it all off, she'd landed in the only place on Earth she'd never planned on visiting— not because of its resident bears, but because of one *human* resident in particular.

Desperation set in like a low-hanging cloud. 'What about your house?'

The woman had no reason to continue to be kind to her, but she did. God love Canada. 'I've already sent two people home to my husband. Both on the sofas. Someone is on their way to get you and drive you into town, ma'am.'

'Can't they just keep on driving me to the nearest city? Something with beds?'

Apparently that thought was *just hilarious*.

The woman laughed. 'The only way in or out

of Churchill is by plane or train. And Winnipeg is a thousand miles to the south.'

Right. Which part of *polar* bear did she miss? Their trusty pilot must really have been desperate to get them out of the air to have landed them in the sub-arctic.

'When will they send another plane, do you think?' she asked weakly.

The woman glanced at her watch and frowned. 'Let's just get you sorted for tonight.'

This wasn't the tightest spot she'd ever been in, though it was the first involving live predators, and the thought of sitting uncomfortably in some waiting room for hours scarcely appealed. Especially when there was no guarantee that she'd get on a flight tomorrow. Or the day after, or the day after.

Her lashes drifted shut.

Desperate times…

'Does Will Margrave still live up here?' she breathed.

He'd moved to Churchill right after the quakes in Nepal. Right after he'd lost Marcella. She'd exploited a working relationship with a clerk at the Department of Foreign Affairs to find out that he'd come home to Canada—come *here*—and then she'd pretended to delete the knowledge from her brain.

'You know Will?'

She'd thought she had. Once. 'It's been a while.'

The airport officer moved immediately towards the phone. 'We don't usually ask Will because his cabin is so far out of town. Kind of isolated—'

Of course it was. Because this day wasn't perfect enough.

'Just try him, please,' she urged. 'Make sure you tell him it's Kitty Callaghan. My full name.'

Kitty glanced out at the airport car park as the woman made her call. The sideways sleet was illuminated against the darkness of the night by floodlighting and she wondered whether the lights might serve as a beacon for any rogue bears wandering past looking for a late-night snack.

'Any airport in a storm…' she muttered.

The airline officer's surprise drew Kitty's focus back across the terminal.

'Okay! John can take you straight there,' she called, hurrying across the shiny floor. 'The taxi ride is on us.'

Suddenly, the police waiting room didn't look quite so bad. Compared to facing Will again. 'Right now?'

The woman glanced at the clock on the wall. 'As soon as your taxi gets here. Looks like it's your lucky day!'

Lucky.

Right.

It wasn't as far as the airport official had implied, as the crow flew, but no self-respecting crow would be out in this weather. The roads gouged through the hardening Boreal sog were slow going, impossible to see more than ten feet ahead of the old SUV that served as one of Churchill's two taxis. It crept along deeper into the forest until they finally pulled up in front of a shadowy cabin with dim firelight glowing inside.

Proper Snow White territory.

'Here we are,' the driver chirped as a hooded figure appeared in the cabin's entrance. He reached across Kitty to open her door and she clambered out into the bitter cold in pumps already soggy from the dash across the airport car park. Immediately her lungs started hurting with the cold.

'Enjoy your stay,' the driver grunted, more to himself than to her, before crunching his vehicle in every ice-topped puddle back up the long drive.

She turned and stared at the shadowy forest cabin.

'Heat's escaping,' a gruff voice called from the open doorway. Then the figure turned and went back inside and only the puffs of mist where his words had been remained, backlit by the light pouring out of the cabin.

Lord…

Time had done nothing to diminish the effect of his voice on the hairs on her neck even as they gathered frost straight out of the sub-arctic air. The gruff rumble turned her insides to jelly just as much now as it had in Nepal. Fortunately, jelly couldn't stand up to the frost in her chest any more than the frost outside it.

Ice was good like that.

The timber protested underfoot as she eased herself up the frosty steps and squelched into the cabin's boot room where she kicked her sodden purple pumps off amongst the rugged footwear already lined up there. The blanket was doing almost nothing to keep her warm, now. But the cabin beyond the boot-room door glowed with warmth and it was enough to lure her over the threshold and back into Will Margrave's world for the first time in five years.

'Help yourself to coffee,' he rumbled from the shadowy back of the cabin, somehow managing to make the friendly offer about as unfriendly as it could possibly be.

'Right,' she said, glancing at the large coffee pot simmering on the old stove. 'Thanks.'

She turned the steaming mug in her numb hands as Will came back into the room, his face still shielded by the fleeced hood of his coat, only adding to her tension. He passed her, wordlessly, and moved into the boot room to shrug the coat off and onto a hook.

Sense memory kicked her square in the belly.

A stranger hearing him for the first time would expect some kind of old salt of the woods. But the man who returned, bootless and coatless, seemed scarcely older than the thirty he had been in Nepal five years ago. His brown hair was messy thanks to his hood and it hung down over his eyebrows. Stubble followed the angles of his jaw up to his cheekbones. He looked as if he should be in a cologne advertisement on a billboard.

Kitty cleared her throat to clear her mind. 'Thank you for—'

'You still okay with dogs?'

The question finally drew his eyes to hers and

she found herself as breathless as the very first time she'd ever gazed into them. *Iceberg,* she remembered. The ethereal, aquamariney, underwater part. An old ache spread below her skin. She had never expected to look into those eyes again.

Will tired of waiting for her answer and broke the spell by moving to the door and opening it wide. Two thick-coated dogs burst in and, behind them, a third. Before Kitty could do more than twist away from them, three more bounded into the room and immediately pounced on her. A seventh held back, lurking by the door.

'Oh…!'

Will barked their names but Kitty was far too busy protecting herself from the onslaught of their wet noses and tongues to pay attention to who was who.

'You keep your dogs in the house?' she cried out of surprise as their assault finally eased off.

Those ice-blue eyes weren't exactly defrosting as the snow on her blanket had. 'You think that they should be out in the weather while you enjoy the comfort in here?'

Well, things were getting off to a *great* start!

'No, I…it's just that you kept them outdoors in Nepal.'

And winters there could be brutal, she was sure. She flinched as doggie claws scraped on her bare arms.

'Churchill isn't Nepal,' Will grunted, then made a squeaking noise with his lips and six of the seven dogs happily mauling her immediately turned and grouped around his legs. The seventh needed some manual assistance from Will.

As he reached around the dog to pull it back, his hand brushed her thigh where her summery skirt stopped. Her skin was too cold and numb even to feel it, let alone to blush at the unexpected contact, but her imagination was in no way impeded by the cold. If anything it was doing double duty standing here in this cabin with Will.

'You're freezing,' Will observed, unhelpfully. 'Not exactly dressed for the conditions.'

A sense of injustice burbled up immediately, as strong as it had once before. Only this time she defended herself. 'Actually, I was perfectly dressed for Zurich where I departed, and for Los Angeles where I should be stopping over by now.'

Two tiny lines appeared between his brows. 'You don't have anything else to put on?'

She shuffled her blanket more firmly around her and wished the fire would do its job more quickly.

'Our luggage won't be released until tomorrow.' Assuming it hadn't been damaged in the fire. As if to make his point, her body unhelpfully chose that moment to shudder from the chill.

Those glacial eyes stared needles into her but then he broke the gaze by sweeping his thick sweater up over his head and tossing it gently to her. 'Put this on, my body heat will help warm you faster. Tuck the blanket around your legs while I get you some socks. And stay by the fire.'

The sweater he removed smelled exactly like the cologne she'd imagined him advertising before. With a healthy dose of man for good measure. Because he'd left the room again in search of emergency socks and because she could disguise it in tugging the thick sweater over her head, Kitty stole a moment to breathe his scent deeply in.

Her eyelids fluttered shut against the gorgeous pain.

All the progress she'd imagined she'd made in the years since Nepal evaporated into nothing as Will's scent filled the spaces between her cells. She'd come to believe she'd fabricated her memory of that smell, but here it was—live and warm and heady—exactly as she remembered.

Except better for the passage of five years.

Like a good wine.

'Folk at the airport must be in quite a spin,' he grunted, returning to the room.

She abandoned the blanket for as long as it took her to tug the large socks on and pull them almost to her knees. Between their heat from below, Will's body heat soaking into her torso and the fire at her back, she finally started to feel the frigidity abating.

From her skin, anyway.

'Not a sight they've probably had before, I guess. The plane was bigger than the entire terminal.'

'Oh, it's happened before,' Will said, easing himself down onto the edge of his dining table, across the small space. About as far back from her as he could be without leaving the room again. 'Courtesy of being the best piece of concrete for a thousand miles.'

Talking about airfields was a close second to talking about the weather. Awkwardness clunked between them like a bit of wood broken loose in the stove.

'I'm grateful you can give me a bed,' she finally said. 'And that you remembered me.'

Those eyes came up. 'You thought I wouldn't?'

She swallowed against their blazing focus. 'Wouldn't remember me? Or wouldn't help me out?'

'Either.'

Thought. Feared. Potato/potahto. 'I wasn't sure whether you'd say yes.'

His grunt sounded much like one of the six dogs that had settled down into every available corner of the room. 'And leave you to the bears?'

She glanced back at him, though he seemed as far away now as Nepal was from this place. The only sounds in the cabin were the crackling of the wood stove and the wide yawn of one of his canine brood. Neither did much to head off her sleepiness.

'So, where should I...?'

That seemed to snap him back to the present from whatever faraway place he'd gone. Remembering Marcella, she imagined.

Sudden sympathy diluted her own tension.

Will had lost so much.

'Second door on the right,' he said, standing aside to unblock her way. 'Bathroom is across the hall. Go easy on the water use—I truck it in.'

The irony of that in a region practically mired in water most of the time—

She picked her way carefully through supine dogs but stopped just as her hand found the door-knob. 'Seriously, Will. Thank you. I wasn't looking forward to sleeping in a waiting room.'

'I'm better than that, at least,' he murmured, holding her gaze.

No *'you're welcome'*. Because she probably wasn't—again. No *'it's lovely to see you again, Kit'*, because it almost certainly wasn't.

Had she really expected open arms after the last conversation they'd ever had?

Will sagged against the door the moment his unexpected guest closed it quietly behind her. How far did you have to go to outrun the past? Clearly, the top of the world still wasn't far enough.

Five years…

Five long years and that time had compressed into nothing the moment Kitty Callaghan had stepped through his front door. The moment he'd answered his phone. His heart hadn't stopped hammering since then. Maybe he should have just let it ring, but he'd recognised the number and he knew that the airport wouldn't have called him at this time of night without very good reason.

It had never occurred to him that the reason would be her.

'Shove up, Dexter,' he murmured nudging the big brown male blocking access to his favourite chair. The dog grumbled but shifted, only to *whomp* down with exaggerated drama a few feet away, and Will sank down into his pre-loved rocker.

Old man's chair, the woman who'd sold it to him had joked.

Yup. And if he had his way he'd still be rocking gently in it by a roasting fire when he'd been in the north long enough to earn that title.

Just him and his dogs… As it was supposed to be.

Last time he'd seen Kitty, she'd been hurriedly tossing her belongings into the back of a dodgy Nepalese taxi and scrambling in after them. Couldn't get off their hillside fast enough. Marcella had wept as her favourite new distraction had departed only ten days into her month-long stay, but he'd kept a careful distance—his heart beating, then, at least as hard as it was now—relieved to see the last of her, certain that Kitty's departure was going to make things with Marcella right again.

He'd worked on their relationship for three more years and it had never been right again.

Which made having Kitty here an extra problem. A man didn't move halfway around the world to escape his past only to invite it right back into his front room. Especially not given how they'd left things.

But… Polar bears.

'It's bigger than it looks back there,' a soft voice suddenly said behind him.

He lurched upright in his chair.

For so long the only voices other than his in this place had been canine. But, somehow, the walls of his cabin absorbed the soft, feminine tones. As if her words were cedar oil and his timber walls were parched.

He struggled for something resembling conversation.

'Plenty of prefabs in town, but I wanted something a little more personal.'

'And private,' she remarked, glancing out of the window. 'It's very isolated.'

Yep, it was. Just how he liked it.

'A mile's a long way in the Boreal. But I have neighbours up the creek and Churchill's only ten minutes away if you know the roads.'

Twenty-five if you didn't.

Did he imagine it, or did her eyes get a shade more anxious at the seclusion? Maybe she, too, was remembering the electricity they'd whipped up between them back in Nepal.

He didn't whip up much of anything these days. No matter who was asking.

It just wasn't worth the risk.

'So…I think I'll head to bed,' she said and, again, it somehow had the same tone as the crackling fire behind him. 'In case they get the plane back in the air early.'

That wasn't going to happen. Churchill was set up for small aircraft—twenty-to-thirty-seaters coming and going across the vast Canadian North like winged buses—and its apron was barely big enough to turn a colossal jet around, let alone get it airborne without a support team. Someone was going to have to fly engineers and safety inspectors up here to help prep the plane for its return flight. And no way were they going to pack a wounded jet full of passengers. Not after they'd taken such risks to get everyone down safely.

But it was two in the morning and Kitty was almost grey with fatigue, so he wasn't about to put that thought in her head.

Time enough for her to find out tomorrow.

'I'll be up at dawn,' he said, instead. 'I'll check on the status for you and wake you in plenty of time.'

'Okay, see you in the morning.'

He turned back to the fire.

'And, Will…?'

Seriously…what was it about a female voice here? His skin was puckering up as if he'd never heard one before.

'Thank you. Truly. I really appreciate the sanctuary.'

Sanctuary. That was exactly what this place had been when he'd bought it. Still was.

Though not so much since his past had stepped foot so confidently in it.

CHAPTER TWO

WILL SQUATTED IN his navy parka and clipped a final boisterous canine to its long chain in the expansive yard, their happy breathing and his murmured words taking form as puffs of mist in the frigid mid-morning air. It hadn't taken Kitty long to track him back there—she just had to follow the excited barks and yips.

Where Will went there were always excited yips. And there were always dogs.

She'd woken pretty late after the adventures of the night before and found two pairs of thermal leggings, a vest, new socks, a scarf, gloves and a pair of military patterned snow boots sitting on the chair just inside the guest-room door. With no idea what she'd find outside, she'd put on all the thermals under her Zurich sundress, the socks and boots, and Will's sweater over the top of the lot. But she'd only had to open the door to the cabin before realising that wasn't going to be quite enough. A spare coat pilfered from Will's boot room helped seal all the heat inside.

Kitty tugged the scarf more tightly around her throat and curled her gloved fingers into the ample sleeves of Will's coat.

Outside the toasty cedar cabin, the air cut into her lungs like glass—even worse than the night before. The temperature had dropped overnight until it was too cold even to sleet, and her throat and lungs burned with her first breaths outside the warm cabin.

Despite the ache, every breath she took seemed to invigorate her. She felt awake and alert and… attuned, though that made no sense. Standing out on Will's front steps cleared her mind in a way that only yoga had before. Except here, she was getting it without the sweating.

The creak of the bottom step last night was more an icy crack this morning, twitching every ear in the place in her direction, before seven sets of pale eyes turned towards her.

'No run for them today?' she called across the open yard.

Will took a while to turn to glance at her. 'Later, maybe.'

He straightened from his crouch and plunged

one hand into the big coat pocket in front of him and rummaged there for a moment. Then he withdrew it, and set about scooping out a generous serving of mixed kibble into each of seven identical bowls recessed into the top of seven identical kennels. As soon as he gave the visual signal, six of the seven dogs leapt nimbly up onto their roof and got stuck into their breakfast.

His left hand found its way back into its pocket and stayed there.

'How did you sleep?' he asked without looking at her.

'Great actually. The darkness out here is very...'

Enveloping. Subsuming. Reassuring.

'Dark?'

She laughed. 'It's very sleep-promoting.'

'That's the forest breathing out,' he replied. 'And low pollution because we're so remote. You'll get used to the extra O2.'

In Nepal, everything had been just a smidge harder because of the reduced oxygen levels in the high-altitude Kathmandu Valley. Did that mean everything would be a bit easier here in the low, flat, sub-arctic forest?

When would 'easy' start, then?

'Shouldn't that make me sleep less, not more?'

'You sleepy now?'

Now? With him crouching there, looking all… good morning? Nope, not one bit.

But she wasn't about to admit that. 'Thank you for the clothes. Just happen to have them lying around?'

Or was she wearing the clothes of some…special friend?

'The supply store opened up early on account of the emergency landing. I headed in there at dawn before it got picked clean by your fellow passengers and got you a few basics. I'll take you in again later if you like, so you can pick out your own gear.'

This kindness from Will…given how they'd left things… She didn't know quite what to do with it.

'I don't really plan on being here long enough to need more.'

The look he gave her then was far too close to the last one he'd ever looked at her with. An amalgam of pity and disappointment.

'They're not going to put you back on a faulty plane,' he warned. 'They'll have to send a replacement, or squeeze you onto the regional services we usually get.'

He returned the kibble tub to the ramshackle

shed that held all his tools and equipment, but as soon as his hands were free again back they went…into his pockets. Only, this time, he caught the direction of her gaze.

'Curious?' he asked, a half-smile on his lips.

Yes… But she was no more entitled to be curious about what was below Will Margrave's pockets now than she was five years ago.

He reached in and drew out a tiny, dark handful of fuzz.

'Oh, my gosh!'

'Starsky's,' he murmured. 'One of three.'

'How old is it?' she asked, staring at the tiny pup. Two slits in its squished little face peered around. Beneath, she got a momentary flash of electric-blue eyes.

Sled-dog eyes.

'Born day before yesterday.'

Two days! 'Should it be away from its mother this soon?'

'Won't be for long,' he murmured. 'Helps to forge a bond with the pup from the get-go. Reinforces dominance and trust with the mother.'

Trust. Yes—that he could just take a newborn pup from its mother even for a few minutes… That she would let him…

'It can't see or hear yet but it has all its other senses,' he said, stroking it gently with his work-roughened thumb. It curled towards him in response. 'And emotional awareness. It will come to know my smell, my voice. The beat of my heart. Knows it's safe with me from its earliest days.'

He did have that kind of voice. All rumbly and reassuring. And that kind of smell. She took a step back against the urge to take in another lungful like last night.

Will returned the pup to its mother's kennel and buried it in under her alongside its two littermates—another black one, and one that was white as the snow all around them with subtle grey mottling.

'So no departing flight this morning, I take it?' she asked as he straightened.

He turned and faced her. 'Let me explain something about bear season…'

'I know, I know… They come for the ice—'

'Not just them,' he interrupted. 'Tourists. Hundreds of them arriving and leaving every day. For eight weeks we're overrun and then we go back to being the sleepy little outpost we usually are. You should be prepared for this to go on for days. Maybe longer.'

Days? Days of this careful eggshells? Of not talking about Marcella or the quakes? Of not mentioning what happened between them five years ago?

'I'll look for somewhere else to stay, then.'

He slashed her that look of his. The one she remembered, the one that used to give her pulse a kick. The *aware* one. As if he saw right through her. And suddenly she regretted the extra layer of thermals. Heat billowed up from nowhere.

'If there was nothing available last night there'll be nothing today. No one else can leave either.'

'Unless someone got eaten by a bear,' she joked.

He didn't dignify that with a comment. But his glare spoke volumes.

Kitty scanned the dog yard carved in amongst the thick Boreal forest and the chains tethering each animal to their cosy little doghouse. That would stop the dogs running wild but it would also stop them running for their lives if a bear happened along.

'How often are dogs attacked by bears?'

The glare redoubled.

'Bears don't kill dogs,' he said irritably. 'Dogs kill dogs.'

She glanced at his pack, so carefully tethered

out of reach of each other. But then she remembered how they'd all piled in together last night quite happily.

'The Boreal wolves are much more likely to attack for territorial reasons. We have a few around here.'

And wolves were mostly nocturnal.

Understanding flooded in. 'That's why you brought them all into the house last night.'

'Most dogs up here live, grow old and die tethered up outside unless they're working. But I lost a young male to a wolf a few weeks back.' He dropped his eyes away from hers. 'He did a good job defending the pack—'

Better than me, she thought she heard him say under his breath as he turned partly away to coil up a length of rope.

'—but his injuries were too severe.'

'The wolf killed him?'

'I killed him,' Will said, his movements sharp. 'The wolf just started it.'

Kitty blinked. He'd had to put his dog down by his own hand?

'I'm sorry, Will. That's rough.'

He shrugged, but it wasn't anywhere near as careless as he probably wanted her to believe.

'The vet flies up from Winnipeg once a month. In between, we have to DIY.'

'Still. You're more about saving lives than taking them.' He'd been rescuing people in need since he was a boy. It was in his blood. He'd been raised by a second-generation search-and-rescue man.

She thought she saw him wince, but he masked it in the turn of his body back towards the cabin.

'Breakfast?' he said, as brightly as his gruff manner allowed.

'You haven't eaten?'

'I don't generally eat before noon,' he said. 'But the fridge is stocked up. Help yourself.'

'Really? You were all about the big breakfast in Nepal,' she murmured, turning to follow him. Then it hit her… Could he not bring himself to have that without his wife?

'Breakfast was Marcella's thing,' he said. 'It meant something to her. Family starting the day together.'

And he'd loved her enough to indulge it.

Sorrow soaked through her. And something else, something closer to…envy. Which pretty much made her the worst person alive. Still hankering for another woman's man, even though that woman was dead.

'Will, I'm so sorry about—'

'Stay as long as you need to,' he said brusquely, gathering up his tools. His words couldn't have been colder if she'd found them lying scattered in the snow. 'You have a fire and food and the best Internet in town.'

'I don't want to be an inconvenience.'

'I'm not planning on being your entertainment,' Will said, gruffly. 'I have work to get on with. There's no inconvenience.'

'No,' she muttered as he turned to wander off. She felt about as welcome as that time in Nepal. 'Of course.'

But as she went to follow him inside, her foot hit a patch of ice and she scrabbled out for the most stable thing she could find.

Will.

He twisted and caught her under one elbow and one armpit—all terribly graceful—and steadied her back onto her feet. The last time he'd been this close she'd stumbled, too. Down some steps in Nepal. That time when Will had caught her hard up against his body, she'd clung to him just as she clung now, and her pulse had rioted in exactly the same way. He'd set her back on her feet, turned and simply walked away, but not before his jaw had clamped in a way that had made her think he'd felt the zing too.

Now, he dropped his hands away from her the moment she was back in charge of her legs, but his eyes fell to her lips and were the last part of him to turn away.

Five years had changed nothing, it seemed.

She still wasn't welcome in Will Callaghan's life.

And his body still said otherwise.

'Take Dexter,' Will called as she headed outside that afternoon all rugged-up. 'If he growls, head back in immediately.'

She paused on the second step and looked down at him working on the motor of a quad bike. 'Why? What will it be?'

'Something bigger than you.'

She'd spent all day indoors—too afraid to go further than dash distance from the phone in case her flight was suddenly scheduled—but by late that afternoon she'd gone a little stir-crazy. Will, good to his word, had busied himself all day and left her to her own devices. She'd poked around the cabin and browsed through his books but there was only so much reading a girl could do. Especially one who usually filled her days to over-flowing with to-do-list. It didn't take long for the tiny cabin surrounded by all these trees to start closing in on her. Enough that she'd temporarily forgotten how wild this place really was despite its modern comforts.

Dexter was stoked to be released from his tether and tasked with being her bodyguard. He galumphed alongside her into the trees, breaking out in wider and wider arcs, sniffing everything he found. Kitty trod carelessly at first but then Dexter's obsession with the Boreal floor drew her eyes downward, too, and she realised what it was she was walking on with her spanking new boots.

Living creatures.

The ground was blanketed with lichens, wa-terlogged plantlets and mosses, all of it jewelled with icicles. Leaves the colour of bruises poked up from between a mossy groundcover so green it was almost yellow. Something white that looked as if it belonged on a reef rather than a forest floor. Some kind of pale parasitic plant, growing hap-pily on anything that didn't fight back, alongside earth-toned fungi piggybacking on a tree's cir-culatory system. Such a perfect natural system working in balance; crowded and chaotic and tangled, but everything was getting exactly what it needed to survive. And all of them poking above last night's snowfall. Now and again, a rare patch of actual ground, something hard underfoot. Not the ground that was made of dirt and went down and down until it hit bedrock—this ground sat on permafrost; a layer of ice, far below, that never managed to thaw, even in summer.

Which would explain the bone-numbing cold rising up through the forest floor into her boots.

She stepped out of the thicker copse of trees to the edge of a clearing and stared into the distance. Orangey brown as far as the eye could see, everything frosted with ice, punctuated by the one-sided Tamarack trees that reached for the sky, and dotted with little swamps of frigid surface water. Really this was just one big, thriving wetland. All of it in soft focus, courtesy of the gentle fog.

She filled her lungs with the cleanest air she'd ever tasted and eased it back out again just as slowly.

It took her a moment to realise that Dexter was growling.

It started low in his long throat and then burbled up and out of his barely parted lips, his tail stiffening and vibrating minutely. He'd turned his stare straight back into the forest, the direction she would have to go to get the short distance back to the house.

Thoughts of all the things out here that could be bigger than her flashed through her mind. Bears, wolves, even caribou could do some damage if they were in the right mood. Or the wrong one. Her eyes darted around for anything with which to defend herself, then she gave up and peered deep into the empty stand of trees she'd just left, breath suspended.

Out of nowhere, a massive flash of grey bounded towards her out of the darkness. She hadn't even seen it lurking! But before she could do more than suck in enough breath for a scream, Dexter's tail lifted from its low, stiff position to a higher wave. Less like an accusing finger and more like a parade flag.

'Jango!' Will stepped out of the shadows behind his dog.

A sawn-off log made for a convenient place to slowly sink down in lieu of collapse. Jango sneezed and bounded off with Dexter to explore, leaving Kitty with only Will to defend her. Even without the firearm he'd slung over his shoulder, she trusted he could do just that. Probably with his bare hands.

He was just that kind of man.

Maybe that was why she'd fallen so hard for him back in Nepal.

'Did I wander too far?' she asked, immediately contrite.

'I needed to give Jango a run to see how her leg is doing, thought I might as well come this way.'

Pfff... 'Worried about the tourist getting lost in your forest?'

'Just worried for my dog,' he corrected carefully.

That brought her eyes around to the hound snuffling around a distant tree. 'What happened to her?'

'She lost a pad to frostbite,' he said. 'Standing guard over an injured hiker last winter.'

Concern stained her voice. 'And she's still healing?'

'She wore a mediboot all summer. It's just come off.'

Kitty couldn't shake the feeling that it was an excuse. Maybe he didn't trust her outside alone. Once a rescuer, always a rescuer.

'It's stunning out here,' she breathed, turning

back to the open stretch where Boreal eased out into more open wetlands. 'Is it all like this?'

'Where it's not tundra,' he grunted. 'Or Hudson Bay.'

He extended his hand to help her to her feet. It took two deep breaths before she could bring herself to slide her fingers into his. But two layers of arctic gloves muted the old zing and she only had to contend with the gentle pressure of his strong hand around hers until he released her.

'Listen, Will…'

His back tightened immediately and he turned away from what was coming. She caught his elbow before he could spin away fully.

'I wanted to…' Lord, how did you start a conversation like this one? *Thank you for telling me your wife died.* 'When Marcella—'

'Sorry it was such a group announcement,' he interrupted.

It was part of what had first drawn her to him, Will's ability to just know what she was thinking. 'Don't apologise. I was so grateful to have heard after everything we'd seen on the news feeds. The quakes…I messaged you. Twice.'

She'd tried to convince her network to let her go to Nepal, to report on the recovery—desperate to see Will still breathing with her own eyes—but in the end the vast numbers of media streaming into the city had only been putting more pressure on Kathmandu's limited resources. Instead, she'd kept herself glued to the feeds coming into her network, looking for the slightest glimpse of Will working with his rescue dogs in the capital. Even as she'd reminded herself why she shouldn't even care. It hadn't occurred to her that either of them faced such risk staying to help out after the first quake.

He winced, but then his gaze lifted and locked onto hers. 'I wasn't really in a position to chat.'

No. He'd just buried his wife.

Metaphorically.

He tugged his arm free and turned to stride away from her along the squishy Boreal floor.

Will's eventual message had shattered her and, as she'd quietly wept, she'd known a deep kind of shame that she was crying not just out of sadness that her friend had died, but also for relief that Will had not.

'How are you doing now?' she risked, catching up with him.

He shrugged, and she supposed it was meant to appear easy. 'That was two years ago.'

'You don't set a watch on losing someone you love. Or on a traumatic event like that.'

He stomped on in silence but finally had no real choice but to answer. 'I'm doing okay.'

'Long way from Nepal,' she prompted, stumbling over a particularly thick thatch of sod grass.

He slowed a little so that she didn't have to scamper after him like an arctic hare. 'I was a bit over mountains. So I looked for the widest, flattest, most open space I could find where I could also work rescue.'

She could well imagine his desire to come home to Canada, too. Back to what he knew. To regroup.

Kitty scanned the distant horizon and the miles and miles of squat flat Boreal stretching all the way to it. 'You sure found flat.'

Dexter and Jango continued to frolic, dashing around and sticking their noses into any space big enough to accommodate one. Given they spent much of their day tethered to their kennels or to a sled, working, this kind of freedom was probably a rare luxury. And sneezing seemed to be Jango's way of celebrating.

'What happened to your dogs in Nepal?' she risked.

His silence was almost answer enough, but

then he finally spoke. 'I had four dogs with me in Kathmandu when the second quake hit, so they survived. I left them behind with Roshan when I left. There was still a lot of recovery work for them to do there without me.'

Only four survivors...

She'd had the privilege of filming most of Will's sixteen dogs out hunting for lost climbers on the Annapurna Mountains, or a pair of hikers caught down in the valleys, or just training out in the field. He'd probably never imagined the horrific circumstances they'd be working in just a few years later. Or that he would lose so many of them in a single event.

'Hard, leaving the four behind...' she probed.

In the silent forest, his voice had no trouble drifting back to her. And when it did it was raw and thick and honest—the Will she remembered from Nepal.

'Harder staying.'

He had suffered immeasurably. Losing his wife, the place he called home, the dogs he trained and loved. Facing death and despair every single day for weeks.

And she was asking him to relive it now.

Heat rushed up from under the collar of her parka. 'Sorry, Will. Blame my enquiring mind…'

It took her a moment to notice that he'd fallen behind her as she picked her way through the moss. She turned. Regret stained his ice-blue eyes, then changed into something more like dark grief.

'No. I'm sorry, Kitty. Your questions are perfectly reasonable. Under the circumstances.'

For the first time since she'd arrived in Churchill he was normal with her. Human. The old Will. The man who had made her breathless with just one look. Faint with the accidental touch of his callused fingers. It was absolutely the right time to go deeper, to wiggle her way in under his protective barriers and hunt for more of the old Will.

Except that Old Will had as little place in New Kitty's life as he did in his own.

The past belonged in the past.

'So, how are you settling in in Churchill?' she asked, to give him a break.

He sighed. 'I keep to myself for the most part. That is reason enough to get noticed up here.'

'I would have thought the north was full of people keeping to themselves.'

'Turns out there are rules to being an outcast. Some social niceties that even hermits are expected to deliver on.' He glanced at her expression. 'I may not have made quite the effort that they were expecting.'

Kitty slid him a sideways glance. 'You shock me.'

On anyone else, that slight twisting of his lips might have been a smile. On Will, it never paid to assume. But her heart flip-flopped regardless. 'Still, the airport lady seemed to think well enough of you.'

'I'm working on it. So what was in Zurich?' he asked, artfully moving the conversation on. 'A story or a man?'

There was nothing in the impassive question to give her pause, yet it did. Maybe it was the irony of *this* man asking her about *other* men. Will Margrave was precisely the reason she'd had no meaningful relationships since the last time she'd seen him. She'd thrown herself into her work for the twelve months after being so rudely ejected from Pokhara, and soon she'd been way too busy escalating her career to entertain more than the most casual of relationships. Too caught up globetrotting and network-hopping and hunting down the big stories.

She'd gone to Nepal in search of a powerful

story, not a powerful attraction. Regardless, afterwards she'd struggled to find a man who could reach the very high bar Will had set.

Perhaps she should thank him for her successful career. He'd given her the shove she needed to be great. Greater.

'I was in Zurich shooting a story about Switzerland's textile industry. Tax haven meets innovation.'

'Industry?' He frowned. 'Doesn't seem like your kind of thing.'

He would say that. The woman he'd met five years ago was into human-interest stories and spectacular natural places, not commercial ventures and tax law.

She pressed her lips together. 'We all change.'

Especially when you were as highly motivated as she had been. Focusing on your career to the exclusion of anything else. 'I'm a foreign correspondent for a Chinese TV network now, CNTV. Their business programmes. Based in LA.'

If by 'based' you meant a postage stamp of an apartment that she rarely ever returned to because she was on the road so much. The world's most expensive storage facility.

'Foreign correspondent makes a little more sense, I guess.'

Was that a compliment or a criticism? It was impossible to tell from Will.

'Nothing wrong with ambition,' she huffed. 'And I go where the stories are.'

Certainly, her career had gone where the promotions were. Hopping from network to network as opportunities presented themselves. The closest she came, these days, to the hobo-like habits of her past.

Lord how she missed the hobo days, sometimes. When her boss's boss was hammering them for a particular angle or cutting a deadline by days it was hard not to long for the freedom she used to enjoy creating her own stories, following her nose, rolling with her instincts.

But she'd traded all that for a steady income and a bigger font on her credit.

'Plenty of stories to be found up here,' Will murmured. 'Maybe you can knock off a few while you wait for your airlift out. Though you might struggle to find something to interest the business set.'

'You don't think cashed-up people want to see polar bears?'

'I know they do. I've escorted some of them

around the district. Though I am curious why you don't seem to want to. Most people would have started nagging hours ago.'

Didn't *want* to? Was that what he thought? The truth was so much more complicated. If she saw a polar bear, how would she stop wanting to see polar bears? Or eagles. Or manatees. Or deserts.

She'd gone for a clean break—and for corporate stories—for a reason.

'I'd like to see a bear,' she breathed on a puff of mist before hurriedly adding, 'Though not out here.'

Again that tiny mouth twist. 'So take a few days to look around.'

Easy for him to say. It wasn't Will's heart aching at the potential of this place. It wasn't his soul trilling to be standing here, knee-deep in lichens and moss. It wasn't his lungs aching with so much more than the coldness of the air around them.

Will wasn't the one who had to leave Churchill the moment her number came up.

She'd already felt what it was like to be banished from somewhere that had rapidly started feeling like her soul home. Why would she set herself up for that again?

'I'm on deadline for the Zurich piece. If I'm not

back in the studio within a few days, this story is going to get cut and aired without me.'

And then who knew what angle it would take? There was no shortage of producers who would love to steal the feature slot she'd fought for. A slot that was scheduled just eight days from now.

Will frowned. 'There's every chance you won't be, Kitty. You need to be prepared for that.'

She chewed her lip. 'Maybe I can cut a rough from here on my laptop, and file that as a starter...'

'I have the best comms outside of the Port because of my rescue work,' Will went on. 'There's a satellite set up out back of the cabin. If you need to be talking to your network in China or sending them rough cuts this is the place to do it from. *Mi data es su data.*'

The man certainly knew how to appeal to a woman's sense of duty... But it didn't stop her chewing her lip.

'Or shoot something entirely else.'

'I'm not sure the business types at CNTV will be queuing up for an exposé on the hidden delights of the fifty-eighth parallel.'

'So don't do it for them, do it for *you*. Call it research if you truly can't bring yourself to just relax and enjoy a few days of downtime.'

Relax? No, not while Will was around. She wouldn't be making that mistake again.

Old Kitty would have chased whatever story excited her and would have told it in whatever way she wanted and then sold it to whoever had the most sympathetic vision. And if no one wanted to buy it she would have whacked it online, free, for the world to enjoy. Because the story was king back then. Money came much further down the list. Back in her idealistic, self-determined, passionate freelance days. Back before she was employed by particular networks to tell particular kinds of stories with particular kinds of agendas for particular kinds of audiences...

Back before New Kitty was born.

But wasn't there some saying about making hay while the sun shone? Or the snow fell, in Churchill's case. She was in the sub-arctic, cut off from the rest of the world, forced to take some time off from her competitive, all-consuming career. If there was a better opportunity to take a few days out of being *Action Kitty* to just remember how it felt to be *Hobo Kitty* she really couldn't imagine it.

And keeping busy...now that definitely held a

heap of appeal. But she made a last-ditch effort to say no.

'Your plane practically fell from the sky, Kit. As excuses go that one is both solid and on public record. You're stuck here for days, and insurance is picking up the tab...'

Kit.

Time had done nothing to dispel the fluttering of her heart when he used the diminutive form of her name. A presumption he'd made five years ago and she'd never been inclined to correct. She'd come to like it. Wait for it, even.

The reality was she was stuck here until tomorrow, if not later. Given how much work she yet had to do on the footage still on her hard drive, she'd be spending most of it in her room, tinkering on her laptop. If she stayed another day—or, God forbid, *days*—she could fill the time with research for a future story. That would keep her busy and out of Will's way.

'I guess that does open up a certain opportunity.'

'And accommodation is free,' he added.

'Not if I find somewhere else to stay.' Which she would, because he wouldn't want her here any more than he had in Nepal. Will was just doing what was expected when a jet liner fell out of the sky in your back yard.

He turned in front of her and stopped her progress. 'You won't find anywhere, not for a few days. Besides you don't need to relocate. You're welcome to stay in my spare room as long as you need it.'

She stiffened her spine and locked gazes. 'I was "welcome" in your home once before, remember?'

And there it was—streaking up his jaw out from under his scrappy beard—a subtle flash of red. The first real evidence that he remembered how they'd parted all those years ago.

Which meant he'd probably be on the lookout for repeats. Which meant she'd be on eggshells for ever, trying to give him nothing.

Everything in her screamed caution not to set herself up for more hurt. A single night was one thing…

'I really don't want to be a bother.'

His lips twisted. 'I'm sure we can give each other plenty of room in a forest this big.'

No, Kitty. You're no bother.

It's fine, Kitty. No trouble.

Relax, Kitty, it's out of your control.

On the scale of denials, Will's effort was nonexistent. Still…maybe picking up after herself and keeping out of his way would be adequate repayment for his dubious hospitality. And her story would get filed. And she'd have some fun reliving the old hobo days.

Win-win.

'Okay. I guess it wouldn't hurt for me to see a few things while I'm here.' She watched him, carefully. 'You know…research.'

The look he gave her then was uncomfortable in the way only Will could make it. As if he saw right through her flimsy excuses. As if he knew exactly how he made her feel and how she *would* feel until she collapsed, emotionally wrung out, into a plane seat and flew far from here.

As if he knew her better than she knew herself.

Pfff. This was Nepal all over again.

CHAPTER THREE

A DAY LATER, Kitty clung desperately to the back of Will's jacket as his quad bike flew them out to the local weir that dammed Churchill River. Will was the closest resident to it, which, apparently, made checking on activity at the weir his responsibility.

'I go out dawn and dusk,' he'd told her as he'd whipped the cover off the quad and hauled it out of the little shelter that kept it frost-free. 'Put the flag up and then lower it again. Check on conditions. I take a different dog each time.'

This morning it was Bose's turn. He'd seemed to know exactly what was happening and his excitement levels were off the chart waiting for them to get moving. Once they got under way, the golden retriever ran full tilt alongside the quad, breaking away to thunder through not quite frozen pools before veering back in to run hard up against Will's left foot.

The quad bounced and slid along the snow-dusted track, crunching through the surface ice formed on puddles and practically flying over every dip and mound. Before long, gripping the back of Will's jacket wasn't enough to keep her firmly in her seat and the wind chill made her gloved fingers ache. So she slid her arms around his waist and dipped her head against the whipping snow and hoped to heaven that he didn't mind the intimacy. Or wouldn't read into it.

Warmer and more secure. And totally necessary.

Yeah, you keep telling yourself that.

The lie got harder to buy every time she breathed a lungful of him in.

As they came up over the final bend, Bose took off ahead of them and bolted down the long strait as fast as his legs could carry him, towards a watchtower overlooking the river.

'Churchill Weir,' Will called back. 'Two hundred thousand cubic metres of rock piled up across the river to control water flow and create a reservoir for boating and fishing.'

Though obviously not so much in the frigid weeks leading up to winter. It was an impressive—but utterly vacant—facility about a mile up from where the Churchill River opened out into Hudson Bay. A mini-marina with boathouse, pontoon berths, first-aid facilities, fire pits, and the three-storey watchtower that served double duty as a lookout for tourists. The steel tower was fully caged in, in the event of a bear-related emergency, presumably. The massive structure could hold fifty people at a pinch.

Just two people and one dog was a pure luxury.

Kitty climbed to the top of the tower while Will checked over the marina and raised a wind-shredded Canadian flag for the day. Bose dived right into the icy river, splashing around like a kid in summer. He found a stick and chased it, tossing it up and letting it drift away on the current before crunching through the ice on the edge of the shore and diving back in after it.

Eventually, man and dog joined her at the bottom of the watchtower.

Around them, the river water churned and surged in the gusty, cold air. Icicles clung to the exposed leaves where it whipped up into a froth amongst the water sedge and polar grass. All around were banks of the rich red stick willow that grew so abundantly up here. Kitty pulled her woollen beanie down more firmly against the icy wind that buffeted her face with invisible needles.

Even the gentle snowflakes felt like blades when they were tossed against her wind-whipped skin.

'Bear!'

She gasped and crouched, pointing to the far side of the weir where a polar bear was in the process of hauling itself out of the river and up onto the bank. It did a full body shake that rippled its massive loose skin, then sauntered out into the middle of the parking area before pausing to think about the world.

It took barely a moment to find them with its beady black eyes once it had turned its nose to the air.

'Inside,' Will ordered, tugging her back into the towering metal lookout. The door closed behind the three of them with a reassuringly heavy clang. They were safe, as long as the bear didn't decide to curl up out there for a nap. People had frozen in less time. Even with two layers of thermals and borrowed down jackets. And even in late autumn.

'Can it smell us?' she whispered.

'No question,' Will said. 'But we won't smell lardy enough to seriously interest it.'

She looked at him quizzically.

'Bears hunt seals for their blubber, not their flesh,' he explained.

'And they can smell it?'

'Two kilometres away, yep.'

'And they don't eat anything but seals?'

'They *can*, but protein is not what they're hungry for. People are way too stringy for them, as a rule.'

Kitty looked at the rangy bear. Its legs were like tree trunks, but its pristine coat hung loose around its frame where body mass was supposed to be.

'He does look hungry,' she said, softly. 'How long since he's eaten?'

'Hard to know. The fact he's swum upriver might be a sign he's got energy from a recent feed, or it might be a sign he's getting desperate. Ranging more widely.'

And every week the ice didn't come was a week longer this bear had to go hungry.

'He looks pretty relaxed.'

'Polar bears love their alone time,' Will murmured. 'They can be social but they like nothing better than striking out alone on the ice and hunting.'

Kitty stole a glance at him.

'What?' he said when he caught the direction of her stare.

'I was thinking that it takes one to know one.'

'Nothing wrong with keeping to yourself,' he said, somewhat defensively.

She went back to staring at the bear from their high position. As her first polar bear went, it wasn't quite what she'd been expecting.

'Why isn't it white?'

'Blubber again,' he said.

She turned from the bear to him.

'High oil content of their winter diet,' he expanded. 'The seal fat stains their coat from the inside out.'

She huffed out her disappointment. '*Seal-fat-yellow*. Wouldn't *that* be a good name for a paint swatch?'

'Give him time.' Will chuckled. 'This fella looks scrappy now but when his moult is finished and he starts feeding up he'll be absolutely breathtaking. You expecting him to tap dance?'

'Skinny and lipid yellow was not what I imagined my first bear would be like.'

'A wild polar bear just hauled himself out of the river right in front of you. Have you really changed that much?'

The criticism bit as sharply as the wind still whipping around them. The implication that nature wasn't good enough for her now.

'It's hard to buy into the *wild* part when he's stretched out in the middle of a marina car park,' she improvised to shift his focus. 'Maybe I should try and see one somewhere a bit less manmade.'

There was a time she'd have gone crazy for a first sighting like that. Back when life was still an adventure. Before everything got so very... structured.

Will snorted. 'I'll take you out there if we get a chance.'

Kitty hopped from foot to foot to stay warm and turned to look at Bose, who had finally ceased his busy laps up and down the stairs and lingered on the metal platform, whimpering piteously.

'Is he upset by the bear?' Kitty frowned.

'His feet hurt on the frozen metal,' Will murmured, bending down to the agitated dog. A moment later he cursed. 'I need your lip balm, Kitty. His feet were wet from his swim. His pads are freezing to the structure.'

The cold must have been affecting her brain; she wasn't usually this slow to connect the dots.

'Your lip balm,' he repeated, more urgently.

'Come on, city girl, you had it out earlier. I know you have it on you somewhere.'

She rifled in the pocket of Will's jacket and produced the little squeeze tube of mint lip jelly. The one arctic-useful thing she'd had on the plane with her.

Will folded himself right down and squeezed a slimy trail of jelly around each of Bose's bonded paws.

He massaged the balm into each pad, loosening the ice's hold on the dog's feet and preventing them from rebonding. Without waiting, Will hoisted him up onto his shoulders. Bose didn't look thrilled to be so awkwardly positioned but it was clearly preferable to being stuck to the watchtower, suffering.

Across the clearing, the bear took offence at all the commotion and hauled itself onto massive feet before wandering off into the distant trees.

'Sorry, big fella,' Will murmured as it departed.

He took his time clanking noisily down the three levels of steel watchtower, balancing the dog precariously over his shoulders and giving the bear enough time and motivation to get well clear, before standing aside so Kitty could unlatch the heavy steel safety gate. As soon as they were out, Will relinquished Bose to the snow-protected ground, and he immediately sprinted over to where the bear had been lying to discover its scent. None the worse for his misadventure.

The surreality of the whole morning caught up with her as they got back to the quad bike and she took a moment to just stare at Will.

'Two days ago I was in one of the most cosmopolitan cities in Europe at a posh product launch,' she said, over the wind. 'It was all suits, caviar, and networking. Now I'm stranded a thousand miles from anywhere with Grizzly bloody Adams, a pack of domesticated wolves and a bear.' She lifted her eyes to him. 'And there's *dog hair* in my lip balm.'

'Welcome to the north.'

Will's easy grin warmed her even as the wind cut bitterly across her face. She stared at the mangled, near-empty little tube of lip balm.

'Maybe you can claim it on insurance,' he chuckled.

But when she continued to blink at him silently he laughed outright, the first time she'd heard that particular aphrodisiac in five long years.

'Could be worse, Kit. Be grateful I didn't ask you to pee on his paws.'

* * *

Had half a decade changed him as much as it had changed her?

Will tethered the last of his dogs after their early afternoon run. Around him their tongues lolled like happy tentacles. All but Starsky, who was still on puppy-guarding duty.

The Kitty Callaghan who'd stepped off that crippled aircraft was highly strung, driven, and more concerned with what her employers wanted than what she did. Half falling out of the sky didn't seem to bother her anywhere near as much as possibly missing a deadline.

Who *was* she?

The woman he remembered was a free spirit, endlessly passionate, full of creativity and curiosity. Nothing had deterred her from pursuing her dream—right up until that last morning, anyway.

She'd blown into Nepal chasing a story about the world's oldest woman and come across his canine rescue unit on her way through. Like the rest of the world, she'd assumed that all alpine rescue in the Himalayas was done by helicopter or by Sherpas with yaks, and she'd assumed that Everest was the only mountain worth falling off. The beautiful Annapurna range—and the team of dogs he ran on them recovering hikers in trouble—were a revelation to her. Just like that, her plans flipped from a week-long visit to a full-month stay.

And his wife had volunteered *them* as hosts. In the too eager way desperate people often grasped at displacement activities. Not that he'd recognised that at the time.

Kitty's spirit—and the way Marcella had responded to it—only highlighted how much vigour his wife had lost since arriving in Nepal eleven months before. Impossible, you'd think, in one of the most spiritual places on the planet. Kitty's enthusiasm for her work had only reminded him how many months it had been since Marcella had picked up her paintbrushes to capture Nepal's gorgeous light. And the way Kitty had interacted with his dogs with zero self-consciousness had reminded him how effortless some things could be. How easy he and Marcella had been with each other in the beginning. Which had only reminded him of how *not* easy things were in Nepal. The place where their young marriage was stripped back in the mountain wind and their flaws and imperfections so brutally exposed.

But having Kitty in their house had been like

having one of his wife's sisters there, and for ten happy days he'd had *his* Marcella back: delightful, happy, engaged Marcella. Pre-Nepal Marcella. More or less.

As a result, he'd spent the first week swinging between gratitude that Kitty's presence had given him his wife back for a bit, and deep shame that it had taken a stranger to accomplish it. In between, he'd struggled not to notice Kitty's many virtues.

He should have known Marcella would decline the moment Kitty left. Hell, he *had* known, and he'd still made the decision to ask her to go. Because having Kitty there day after day had seemed a much greater risk to his marriage than Marcella's wildly fluctuating moods.

As it had turned out, the real risk had been lurking deep below the earth.

'Step up, Bruiser,' he commanded, and the biggest and blackest of his team moved up to stand patiently in front of his squatted thighs.

He checked his wheel dog over quickly, paying particular attention to the place between his pads where chunks of rock ice sometimes got caught after a snow run, and then tethered him to his kennel, and gave Bruiser a full body rub, mussing his thick coat and getting into all his favourite places. He let himself out of the yard and scuffed his boots as he came up the stairs to shake them free of slush.

He felt the heat the moment he entered the cabin. When he went out on long training runs, his fire generally burned right down to ash coals making the house cool on his return, but Kitty had clearly kept it stoked while she'd passed the morning, and—his nose informed him as he shrugged out of his coat—she'd made soup. In his kitchen. Not from scratch, but she'd hunted and gathered a couple of tins for her lunch and left the rest simmering awaiting his return.

His muscles softened. It had been a long time since someone had looked out for him like that. Thoughtful, but not over the top. If he'd walked in here and found her in the kitchen waiting for him in an apron with a hot bowl of stew, a slab of freshly buttered bread and a smile, he might have had to walk right out again. But this—just the casual kindness of a stoked fire and simmering canned soup left—*this* he could handle. And almost get used to.

Which was reason enough to not let it happen again. She would be back on her way any day now and he would be back to his solo existence. The one he'd worked so hard for. And she would get on with her life unimpeded by him.

'Kitty?'

He stood by the fire and listened out for her reply from the back of the cabin. Nothing. He took a moment to look out of the kitchen window to the forest yard behind them. Also nothing.

Surely, she wouldn't have gone exploring again alone? Not after all his warnings about taking a dog for security. His heart began to thump. The fear was as instinctive as the presumption of stupidity. He'd lost enough in his life for the former, and rescued enough stranded tourists for the latter.

A quick glance confirmed her military-patterned boots were still sitting in the boot room so wherever she'd gone, she'd gone there inadequately dressed for the conditions.

He opened the front door and stuck his uncovered head out into the silent Boreal. 'Kitty?'

Nada.

Okay, now his heart started hammering in earnest. He jogged back past her boots. Maybe she'd had a call from the airline and forgotten them in her rush to depart for the airport. He scanned the living room; maybe she'd left a note he was yet to find. Or maybe she'd just gone and would send him a thank-you card later.

Or not at all… It wasn't as if they were friends or anything.

He nudged the door to his spare room open, feeling guilty for intruding on her space. When did it start to feel like *her* space? It only took a nanosecond to confirm that her belongings were all still there.

Okay, that only left the frigid outdoors…bootless.

Immediately, old memories surged up and chilled his blood. She wouldn't last an hour.

Why the hell hadn't he taken her with him on the dogs' training run? He wouldn't make that mistake again. He wouldn't leave her for a moment. She would have to beg him for some privacy.

Maybe if he'd been that insistent with Marcella—

But as he rushed back through the cabin, a noise from the shadowy far end got his attention. He skidded to a halt and frowned up into the darkness. There was nothing at the far end of the hall but a coat closet, where he kept a mountain of winter wear packed in tight. He did a fair impersonation of a wolf, tilting its head. *All the better to hear you with...*

Then he moved.

'Will!'

Kitty's outrage as he flung open the coat closet door smacked headlong into the rising panic he'd been so woefully managing.

'What the hell are you doing?' he cried.

'Working!' she shouted back as she stumbled out of the closet.

'What?'

She pulled one earphone out from under her dark curls and held up the compact, professional microphone. A cable ran from them both down to the laptop perched on the floor of the closet.

'I spent the morning scripting the Zurich story,' she said. 'Now I'm laying down a narration track to edit the story to.'

Her phone glowed bright in the darkness, illuminating a bunch of text.

'In the closet?'

Okay, he hadn't been quite this hysterical for a long time. He fought to get his emotions under control.

'You have a lot of coats,' she defended weakly. 'It's perfect.'

He stared at her a moment longer before turning and walking away—and the adrenaline left his body as swiftly as it had come.

'It's an old field trick,' she called, ditching the mic and earphones and scurrying after him. 'In the absence of a recording booth you make an igloo out of bedcovers or use a closet full of clothes to absorb the stray sound. Yours was perfect. Why do you have so many coats?' she puffed.

The image of Kitty smothered beneath a mountain of quilts recording her damned audio threatened to morph into an image of her trapped beneath a mountain of mud and rubble. Which he knew was both illogical and impossible, but it wasn't his logical brain pumping anxiety hormones through his body. It was his most basic lizard brain.

The place where all his fears had set up camp.

Kitty was not Marcella. Nor any of the hundreds of Nepalese he'd helped recover from their rocky tombs.

'Will…?'

She trailed him at a careful distance, reminding him of Tanner when he'd first come into his team. The rangy dog had been so poorly kept by his previous owner he'd looked for betrayal and violence in every shadow. Will hated that he was making Kitty look like that, but he would deal with self-loathing later. Right now he was all about breathing.

He sagged down onto his rocker. Its familiar feel and motion helped him to calm down.

'I'm sorry if I worried you,' she began. But it was clear that she thought his reaction disproportionate to her crime. And inconsistent with a lifetime of courage under fire hauling other people out of danger.

Which meant she knew what this was *really* all about.

He hated her seeing him like this.

'Sorry,' he choked, shaking the awful images free. Trying to. 'Another time, another place.'

'Does this happen often?' she asked gently, knowing better than to touch him. Or to offer him her pity.

His breathing seemed to be getting harder, not easier. He tried to relax his grip on the timber arms of his chair.

'Nope.' Because he didn't let it. 'Special one-time performance.'

'It's okay, Will. After what you went through—'

'You have no idea what I went through,' he snapped.

How could she, when he'd told no one? But she wasn't about to be snarled off the topic. That was something else he remembered about her. Tenacious as hell. And endlessly patient. It was what made her so good at her job.

'I'd be happy to listen. If you want to talk.'

Talk? Why would he do that? He'd worked so hard to put it all away from him. So he could function.

Why would he want to relive the urgent drive back to Pokhara when he'd heard about their village? Back to the temporary field camp he'd convinced Marcella to join their neighbours in rather than go back into their big house up the hill while the aftershocks were still coming so frequently. Finding half a mountain piled up in that field instead, wet and dense. House gone. Neighbours gone. Dogs gone.

Marcella gone.

The loyal woman who'd followed him to Nepal and been so very miserable there.

All he'd had, then, were the clothes he'd stood in, the single team of exhausted dogs he'd been out working with when the landslide had hit, and his work.

There was always work.

'It's okay to miss her,' Kitty tried again.

What could he say to that? Better that she believe this was just a simple case of grief. Or post-traumatic stress. Better that she not know what was really going on. That maybe if he'd protected his own family in Nepal rather than other people's, then a beautiful woman would still be alive today. Or that if he'd just manned up and accepted reality, Marcella never would have been standing in that field that day. Or even been in Nepal. She would have been back home in the US, with her family.

Safe.

Alive.

'I just need a minute,' he gritted, still struggling against his own lungs.

She stepped back and considered him. Then spoke carefully. 'I've been cooped up in that closet for too long. Think I'll take a quick walk.'

But before she could do more than step towards the boot room he found the air he needed to remind her, 'Take a dog!'

CHAPTER FOUR

TAKE A DOG...

Even in the midst of an obvious personal crisis, Will had enough sense to keep her safe. Kitty stomped her boot more fully on as she stepped outside, his coat clenched in her fist. Giving him the space he needed. Giving him some privacy.

And some dignity.

She wouldn't need a dog because she wasn't going to go further from the cabin than she could dash back to in thirty seconds. Just because she didn't want to humiliate Will by watching his meltdown didn't mean she was going to leave him to do it completely alone. If he needed her, she was going to be close by. She owed him that much.

Despite everything.

She'd been patient and understanding, and respectful of his loss—his failure to reply to her shocked messages—until, eventually, she'd just accepted his need for privacy. And accepted that it was going to have to be enough just to know that he had survived.

She didn't get to know if he was okay.

She shrugged more fully into her parka and then let herself into the dog yard where all seven of Will's dogs guarded the entrances to their kennels, snuggled inside or kept watch from the flat roofs.

'Hey, Jango,' she said, approaching the closest. The female snow dog did what she always did when she got over-excited—she sneezed. Full-body sneezes. It was kind of her thing. As if all that excited emotion had to get out somehow. She stood on the roof of her kennel and wiggled and sneezed as Kitty ran her forked fingers through her thick, pale fur. Her light eyes closed blissfully at the contact. The patch of pink pigment on her otherwise black nose was the only distinctive marking Jango had but it made her easier to identify amongst the three almost identical huskies in Will's pack.

Jango's closest neighbour reached to the furthest lengths of his tether and strained forward for his own pat, dodging and weaving like the clown he was to get attention.

'Yeah, I see you, Ernie.'

She visited every dog in the yard. Buying Will

some time. Filling hers. Every dog had its own personality, even tethered as they were. Dexter was the serious one, Bruiser was the surly one. Bose was just as happy tied up as he had been running alongside the quad yesterday. Tanner kept a wary distance and Starsky... Well, she was a new mum, exhausted from raising her pups. So Starsky perpetually looked half asleep.

But every dog had one thing in common, and that was the focused excitement when Will walked into their yard.

Starsky blinked wary eyes up at her, so Kitty squatted to reduce the threat to her pups and murmured in her most comforting voice, 'Hey, girl...'

The side of her kennel thudded, rhythmically.

'How are your babies doing, huh?'

There was no way she was going to reach in there with her hand as she'd seen Will do, but Starsky was obliging enough to roll onto her side submissively, which made the three balls of fluff tucked in tight around her belly easier to see. Two black and one a stark white explosion of fur. The white one opened its tiny mouth wide in a massive, red yawn.

She'd never been particularly clucky—you had to spend time with people in order to spend time around their babies and she was always way too 'busy' to make friends—but something soft and squishy rushed through her at Starsky's beautiful nurturing as the dog nudged each pup with her nose to reassure them they were safe.

And it softened further that Starsky understood she was safe with *her*.

'Want to hold one?'

Will's voice behind her was at once full of awkwardness and apology. Kitty spun to face him, scrutinising him closely for signs of distress.

'Am I limited to one?' She smiled. As gently as she could, yearning to see the same expression in Will's eyes that she'd seen in Starsky's. The knowledge that he was safe with her.

'Thank you, Kitty,' he said, though it obviously cost him. 'For giving me the space. That kind of took me by surprise.'

Old Kitty would have pressed him, then; to force her help on him. But she didn't, she just smiled and nodded.

So maybe she had changed, some.

Will squatted next to her and reached carefully in, murmuring words of security and strength to Starsky and drawing out a pup in each hand. He kept a black one and passed her little yawning friend to Kitty.

'Open your jacket,' he said. 'Tuck it in close so it can feel your heartbeat.'

Surely that wouldn't fool even an inexperienced newborn? Not while smell and texture and pulses were such a massive part of its existence. Though, her heart was practically tap dancing simply for being near Will so maybe the pup would not notice much difference after all.

She unzipped her jacket low enough to tuck the white pup snugly between her breasts where it was close and warm against her thermals.

'Who is his father?' she murmured low enough to reassure the pup and its mother, who was keeping the closest of eyes on her babies.

'Diego, the dog I lost to the wolves.'

'Oh,' she said sadly. 'What an awful shame.' She peered down. 'You'll never know your daddy, little one.'

'He'll know me,' Will murmured. 'I'll sub for Diego.'

Will would make a good substitute father. Or the real thing. He just had that kind of temperament—patient, reliable, confident. Once, she'd entertained thoughts of what it would be like to have children, but she never could quite picture who the father might be. And when finally she did meet someone she *could* picture, he was only free to be daddy to someone else's kids. She'd put that thought away from her and focused on raising a career instead. As a result, she didn't really do soft and squishy any more. But as it thrummed through her, it was nice to know it was still in there.

Somewhere.

'Want to name him?' Will asked, not quite meeting her eyes.

'Really?'

'Go for it.'

She studied the little white fluff-ball down her front. Coat as white as snow, eyes as dark as night, tongue as red as blood.

The old folktale came leaping to mind.

'Grimm.'

Will turned his curiosity to her.

'I can't really call a boy dog Snow White, can I?'

Will smiled. 'Well, you could. We're a gender neutral team, but I like Grimm. It suits.'

'What about yours?'

Will drew the dark pup out of his pocket and looked at its underside then back at its face. Deep into its eyes. 'She's "Zurich".'

Kitty snapped her gaze up to his. She fought against the warm little glow and reminded herself that it was just as likely that he'd run out of names in the easier part of the alphabet.

'Did you just name a dog after me?' As if it weren't an honour. As if it weren't the greatest, *Will*est gesture.

'Dark hair, big grey eyes.' He shrugged as her heart thrummed. She did everything she could not to let him see the effect his gesture had on her. Maybe he misread that as offence because he retreated almost immediately from the intimacy.

'Kind of bitey,' he said, deadpan. 'Plus I don't have a "Z" in the team yet.'

The humour was the lifeline she needed to haul herself out of the dangerous swill of feelings. She wrapped both hands around it and held on.

'What about that one?'

He named the other black one Midnight.

She gave Grimm a final caress, leaned in and tucked him securely back under his mum. Then she pushed onto her feet. 'What will you do with them when they're bigger?'

Keep them, she hoped.

'Depends on their super powers.'

'Their what?'

'Every dog here has something it's particularly good at. Something fitted to a specific role in the team.' He returned Zurich to Starsky's care, too. 'Three of the four huskies are just runners—that's their super power—but Jango and the other dogs do double duty with other jobs.'

'What other jobs?'

'Bose and Jango are live trackers. Starsky and Tanner are cadaver dogs.'

Will's reality came home to her. This was his job—death and loss were everyday to him whether or not he encountered them every day.

'That's why they're different breeds,' she realised. Like the mixed team he'd had in Nepal. 'You train them every day?'

'Partly for harness fitness; partly to reinforce their individual places in the team and mine at the head of it.'

Jango leapt up and pressed muddy paws onto Will's clean coat. Kitty braced herself for his reaction, but he didn't even flinch. He just stepped away. For a man who'd been such a wreck fifteen minutes earlier, his composure now was impressive. That was how she knew Will Margrave best—in control.

'These are northern working dogs—not city

dogs who have to live with kids and walk in busy streets and play well with others. Their strong personalities are part of what make them good at their jobs, so I want them to be able to express them, not water them down.'

She ran her eyes over the yard. 'I wish workplaces operated like that.'

Her senior producer obviously did not subscribe to the Will Margrave school of management. Mei-Xiu had no idea how to harness individual talent the way Will did with his dogs. For Mei, team achievements were significant only in as much as they reflected on her. Every day, she looked to see who might be growing better or brighter than she was so that she could quietly temper their success.

That was how Kitty had first become *foreign* correspondent. Mei-Xiu had seen her potential and taken pains to banish her from the CNTV kingdom entirely. All the way to Los Angeles where she was officially out of sight and out of mind. How disappointed Mei must have been when the wider access had only resulted in better content—and more of it—from her professional rival. Though Mei was nothing if not adaptable and always managed to find a way to claim partial credit for Kitty's work.

'Is that your way of saying you wish everyone would just toe your line?' he said.

She turned to him and lifted her chin, taking extra care to keep the thump out of her voice. 'You admire unleashed personality in a dog but not in a person?'

His eyes darkened. 'I didn't say I didn't admire it. Confidence and capability are always appealing.'

A warm glow kindled to life. Finding her traits appealing was just a pained heartbeat away from finding her appealing.

'I just think it's obvious where Kitty Callaghan would fit in a team,' he went on, and the glow sputtered out. 'At the front.'

'Says the man who gets the free ride while his team do all the hard work.'

His smile, when it came, was like an unexpected burst of sunshine through the ever-present Churchill cloud and the words dried up between them, replaced by something that defied language. Something that busied around them like a hundred arctic bumblebees—soft and caressing—and had to be felt, not heard.

Until Will shook them away.

'So, listen, I have this thing on this afternoon...

in town. I was going to leave you home for it but after—' He caught himself, glanced at the cabin, and changed tack. 'But I've changed my mind. How about you come in with me?'

Thing? That could mean anything from a supply run to a date. Something told her Will wouldn't find it hard to find female company even in a Y-chromosome-dominated town, in which case she absolutely was not about to hang around like a third wheel.

Not again.

She didn't need to be looking around town, she needed to be finishing her rough cut. But that shadow behind Will's gaze said that he wasn't about to let her out of his sight and, truth be told, she wasn't in a hurry to spend any more hours alone in a room.

'I guess there is only so much time a girl can spend in the coat closet,' she joked. 'I'll have a look around for the afternoon while you do your... *thing*. Get my own coat, maybe.'

Her luggage had been delivered but it still didn't have much of sub-arctic use in it.

Will frowned. Actual, genuine disappointment.

'I've kind of grown used to you getting about in

mine.' Blue ice seemed to swill behind the fringe of his lashes. 'It suits you.'

'In an alternate universe where people wear sacks, maybe. I wouldn't mind something a little more…tailored.'

'Tailored?' He blinked at her. 'Seriously… What happened to you this past five years?'

'I grew up, Will. Had to happen sooner or later.'

His regard grew uncomfortably long before he finally spoke again. 'Not really sure what will be left on the shelves after one hundred and sixty freezing passengers have stripped the place of emergency gear, but no harm in looking, I guess. I'll take you somewhere less known. Then you can come with me on my thing when you're done.'

On his date? No, thank you.

'I'll make my own way back—'

'I'll bring you home,' he cut in.

There it was again. The idea that he was responsible for her. Or that she was answerable to him.

Still, who knew how long she would have to wait for one of Churchill's two taxis…?

'I'd like to see more of the town,' she stated for the record. 'As long as I'm not in your way.'

'No more than here,' he grunted.

CHAPTER FIVE

WILL MIGHT AS well have rolled himself in seal blubber and gone to hang out with the polar bears in the conservation area. He was handsome, mysterious and half soaked in *eau de unattainable* and, unsurprisingly, everywhere they went in town, thick-lashed eyes followed him.

The local ones just slid sideways as he passed, as if Churchill's women knew from experience not to stare outright. But the out-of-towners didn't know him, so those gazes—and there were many of them—sat on a spectrum anywhere from *appreciation* to outright *invitation*.

Will seemed oblivious to it all—or uncaring— but Kitty saw and felt every glance.

As he'd warned, the Trading Post had been thoroughly picked over by the rest of her flight and the tourists in town, running their stock disappointingly low. But Will had bundled her back into his truck and driven her to the fringes of town before pulling in at a supply company that seemed to specialise in water pumps, fishing gear and woollen balaclavas.

Kitty glared back at him as she entered.

'Don't judge a book by its cover,' he said.

Clearly, while the Trading Post was busy with visitors to Churchill, *this* was the store of choice for locals. It was packed to bulging with every comfort for northern life—everything from organic eggs to snowmobiles.

'Coats are down the back,' Will said.

At first she was blind to anything but the swathes of green-grey and bark-brown. But if drab was the look she was going for then she'd keep on wearing Will's enormous, thick parka. It didn't take her long to find her way to the back of the building. Stores were run by people, and people were the same wherever you went—they put the things they wanted you to see up front and kept the other things—the special things—tucked away somewhere safe. Like gems just waiting to be discovered.

Bingo.

Kitty stepped beyond the rack of functional coats into what was probably a 'staff only' area, drawn by the flash of a colour she didn't really have a name for. It was halfway between orange and cherry, kind of metallic in look with a big fluffy grey hood. Quilted yet svelte, the goose-down coat drew in at the front and waist courtesy of a series of black straps that ran the length of the extra-long coat like rungs of a ladder. Kitty shrugged out of Will's big, drab parka and into the candy confection, taking care not to miss a single strap.

It was patently ridiculous. But it was completely perfect. And it fitted her like the matching gloves she would sell a kidney to find back there.

Sometimes, a girl just wanted to stand out.

'Got that in on special order for someone,' a smoker's voice behind her said, 'then she didn't like the colour.'

Kitty turned to face the shop's owner. He had a woollen, knitted bear mask on around his weathered face. Complete with adorable little curved ears. She ignored it entirely. In polar bear central a Grizzly just didn't seem that out of place.

'I *love* the colour.'

'I guess you'd need to.' He chuckled past his bear nose. 'Fits you real well, though.'

She ran her hand down the shimmery surface.

Yes, it did. Plus it was the most feminine she'd felt since stepping foot on the A340 in Zurich.

It took her a moment to come to terms with the very simple reality: She wanted to look pretty. *For Will.* And she wasn't the slightest bit sorry about that. She was tired of looking like a reject from the military Goodwill around him.

'You back there, Kitty?'

In the mirror, he appeared behind her as if she'd conjured him. She spun to face him, sliding the big hood up to half subsume her face.

He stumbled to a halt and stared at her.

She plunged her hands into the coat's deep pockets and struck a pose. 'How do I look?'

Will took a moment to clear his throat. 'Like a tourist.'

Clearly an insult coming from a local but, given he wasn't taking his eyes off her, she wasn't going to lose much sleep over that.

Something deep within her cheered. 'It feels fantastic.'

Blue eyes followed her hands as they traced up and over every metallic curve. The soft fur lining of the hood brushed her cheeks like a caress.

'I'll take it,' she called to the storeman. 'Can I wear it out of here?'

Given the price tag, and given he'd been stuck

with it for who knew how long, she could probably walk out of here naked but for the coat and the man wouldn't raise an eyebrow. Will fell in behind her as she paid for it, some batteries and a simple pair of woollen black gloves to replace the thick, feel-nothing mitts he'd loaned her on the first morning.

When the transaction was complete she turned back to a still-silent Will and gave him her biggest grin. 'Yay!'

Maybe if she was excited enough for both of them she could counter his apparent sudden gloom.

Or was he just thinking of having to step out in public with a human hotdog?

'I guess I don't have to worry about losing you in the forest again,' he quipped as he opened the store's door for her.

See? Feminine. He hadn't opened it for her on the way in.

Kitty tamped down a triumphant smile. 'Technically you don't have to worry about me in the forest *at all*. I'm a big girl, I can look after myself.'

'If this is what happens when you shop for yourself, I'm not so sure.'

Yeah, yeah... She'd be offended if not for the fact that he was still sneaking sideways looks at her.

He stopped them next at a busy café in the heart of town. It was filled to overflowing with tourists but seemed equally popular with the locals.

'Best coffee in town,' Will had said as he pulled into the car park crowded with buses and pulled his collar up higher before shoving open the driver's side door.

Inside, the place was festooned in cobwebs, as were some of the staff. Ghouls, zombies and witches everywhere, with a carved pumpkin candle on every table. A portly man served at the coffee counter clad in a black onesie with a white skeleton painted on it and a pretty young girl with a bloodied hatchet through her blue hair worked the register. It was hard to know if the hair was part of the costume or not, but its vibrant colour lent her tan skin a luminescence that only made her lovelier.

'It's Halloween.' Kitty spoke aloud, though she hadn't meant to.

Will slid her a sideways glance. 'You think?'

What was it about this man that he could make her feel as callow as a teenager with a few short syllables...?

'Halloween's not really a thing in Australia,' she explained as they joined the back of a long-ish coffee queue. 'I didn't make the connection.'

But now the grizzly bear in the supply store made so much more sense.

'I'm wondering if you can still call yourself Australian if you haven't been to the place in years,' Will said, catching the skeleton's eye and tossing his chin in greeting.

'If that were true I'd be stateless, the way I move about.'

They shuffled forward in the line by one. She glanced around and realised how easy it was to tell the locals from the visitors. Like her, the tourists had bright, clean, brand-new snow gear. And they outnumbered the locals ten to one.

'Gathering no moss?' he said.

'Building a career.'

'And what about a life?'

'Churchill. Nepal. Montana. Newfoundland...' She counted them off on her de-gloved fingers. 'You want me to go all the way back to your childhood?'

In other words: *Pot. Kettle. Black.*

He turned a baleful expression on her as they approached the front of the queue. 'I had a life.'

His use of the past tense dug in right under her ribs. 'And I've got one. It's just different from yours. What's wrong with rolling stones, anyway?'

He turned those icy blues onto her. 'What's wrong with moss?'

The skeleton greeted him by name and slid a freshly prepared coffee and a folded piece of paper straight to him before taking Kitty's order. Like some poorly executed intelligence drop. The business of the following minutes forced a pause in the conversation but it also took some of the heat out of it.

'I think we can both say that we've done and seen things that most people never would,' she said when at last they were free of the noisy crowd. 'That's common ground, right?'

His eyes grew bleak. 'True enough.'

The silence was almost less bearable than the conversation.

'So what is it you're doing in town today?' She rushed rather than endure it.

'Bear sweep,' he said, simply.

She blinked at him. 'A what?'

'It's Halloween.' *As she'd so astutely reminded him.* 'We sweep the town and then set up a perimeter around it with our trucks so that the kids can safely go trick-or-treating.'

Kitty paused with her coffee halfway to her lips. The thought of grumpy Will Margrave involved in something quite so…civic…managed to nudge out the mental image of children in costumes finding themselves nose to nose with a hungry polar bear. Churchill kids grew up into Churchill adults and so the healthy respect the locals had for the bears had to start somewhere. But it had simply not occurred to her that candy-toting kids and hungry carnivores could not possibly share the same streets.

What a story this would make…

'Like circling the wagons,' she realised.

'Pretty much. With patrols armed with tranq guns and a chopper keeping watch overhead.'

'All for one night of candy and costumes?'

'For one night of community bonding. And of freedom. These kids see little enough of it.'

She considered him for only a moment, then made her decision. Shopping could wait.

'Okay if I tag along?' She reached into the back seat and snaffled up her video camera.

He'd driven her past Churchill's packed and multifaceted community centre—school, leisure centre, health centre, playground, library, swimming pool, ice rink, theatre and gym—but she'd assumed the indoor *everything* complex was like so many towns with sub-zero climates… All about the weather.

Here, it had the primary purpose of keeping Churchill's kids safe from bears, and a town where the children perpetually moved from their homes to virtual enclosures for their own safety made for a really interesting angle.

He glanced at her equipment then back up to her eyes. 'Is your interest professional or personal?'

'Professional. Of course.'

Although, if there was anything sexier than rescuing people from mountains it had to be protecting little children from bears, right? She wasn't going to miss out on the chance to watch Will help do that.

'Or I could just strike out on my own?' she suggested, smiling.

Will glared and she started filming.

'These are our streets,' he said, waving the

hand-drawn sketch he'd received in the café in the vague direction of her camera. 'Between now and dusk we just move through town along with dozens of others, checking every nook and cranny. In about two hours, we'll move to a spot on the edge of town to form the perimeter barrier and the armed patrols will take over down here.'

And, so, she trotted along a few metres behind Will dressed in her fine new coat with her camera as he moved up and down four of Churchill's streets while the sun sank lower on the horizon. The town was a curious mix of traditional Canadian architecture and bright timber cabins all mixed in amongst the prefabricated industrial-style buildings you'd expect in a port town. Trucks, SUVs, quad bikes and tourist buses parked wherever they could get a spot. More than one yard had used discarded rubber tyres from the massive vehicles that moved around out on the tundra to create a raised garden bed for things that just couldn't grow in permafrost. They painted them brightly, adding to the colourful mosaic of street art.

It reminded her of the ubiquitous, bright prayer flags in Nepal.

She glanced at Will and wondered if he'd ever made the connection.

'So if we find a bear,' she interrupted her own thoughts and pointed the camera at him, 'what do we do?'

He shrugged. 'Shut yourself in the nearest vehicle and call the Bear Patrol.'

She hit the brakes. 'I'm serious, Will.'

He stopped and turned back to her. 'Standard procedure. Everyone up here leaves their vehicles unlocked for exactly that purpose. But don't worry, with this many people swarming around I don't think any self-respecting bear will stick around. The issue is that a bear caught short at sunup may have crawled under a house to sleep until dusk and not be aware.'

So, that was why he kept giving the undersides of houses a burst with his torch. She took extra care to capture him doing that.

'Bears and people co-exist well most of the time,' he went on, after straightening from another one. 'It's only when something unexpected happens that things get sticky. They aren't out looking to pick a fight, they're just scavenging.'

Dirt-covered scavengers hiding under houses...

Kitty sighed. 'I'm seriously going to have to re-assess my mental image of polar bears.'

'Wait until you see them in their own habitat instead of ours. I'm not sending you home until you have the full picture.'

She peered up at him as they turned up a par-ticularly shadowy street. 'The airline is already keeping me captive. You planning on adding to that?'

'Got something better to be doing?'

She blinked back at him. The truth was she had nothing lined up for after the Zurich story. She'd been looking, but nothing had captured her in-terest or her imagination. Which pretty much summed up her life these past weeks.

Months, maybe.

Will folded himself down to peer under a porch. Instinct told her that there was nothing that he couldn't handle, but they weren't really prepared for a skirmish with a three-hundred-kilo wild an-imal.

'So what do the professionals do with a *hangry* bear?'

'Trap it. Airlift it back to the conservation zone and leave it with some food as an incentive to stay put.'

Kitty's heart squeezed. Another story danced seductively in her mind. Oh, the stories she might film, here, rather than talking about tax evasion and textiles...

Sigh.

'And if it comes back for another go at the flight-with-food upgrade option?'

'Repeat offenders spend a dull few weeks in the holding facility before they're relocated one hundred miles from here. So they associate town with the negative experience and the wild habitat with the positive one.'

'Are they that easily persuaded?'

'Bears are like people,' he murmured, this time straight down the lens. 'They just want food and shelter for their families. To keep them safe. To survive.'

The street's shadows seemed to infect Will's gaze. Kitty tugged her furry new hood more firmly around her face against the stinging, frozen wind.

'Come on,' Will said, noticing. 'Time to circle those wagons.'

Halloween was what had pulled him out of the deep morass that he'd been trapped in when he'd first arrived in the north. Little children—vulnerable, distracted—wandering the streets of this remote, hostile place, trusting that the grown-ups would have their backs. He'd almost pulled out when he'd discovered what he'd signed up for, that he was expected to keep *kids* safe against *bears*—the man who couldn't keep his own wife safe against dirt—but he was Churchill's new Search and Rescue man, refusing to protect their young just wasn't an option.

And so he'd come. And he'd driven home again with the first real hope he'd felt in months. Seeing their optimistic little ghoul-painted faces, seeing those smiles and knowing that all he had to do to keep them safe was *be there*...with his lights on... It had reminded him of how many lives he had saved by being there with a dog or two in tow.

Even if he hadn't managed to *be there* when it had counted for his wife.

He pulled up in his assigned spot on a rise above town, thirty feet left of Mark Quelot in his shiny new SUV and right of Dom Brennan's battered old delivery truck, his headlights shining away from town to create a bright barrier no lurking bear would be foolish enough to walk towards. Kitty clambered into the truck's back seat and locked her camera off to film on full zoom down into town where little scarecrows and mini-vampires and superheroes started wandering from house to house ahead of the early sunset. Witches and dragons and werewolves. But no ghosts. No zombie brides. And definitely no polar bears.

Kitty freed the camera and turned it on him on the realisation. 'No one wears white.'

In the warmth of the truck's cab, she had dropped the grey fur hood that had matched her eyes so perfectly. But losing the hood only meant the coat's rich sheen could spill up onto her pale skin, giving her a warm glow even in the gloaming light of dusk. Fortunately, the camera relieved him of the burden of not staring.

'No white,' he murmured, doing his best to pretend the camera wasn't there. He shuffled more comfortably behind the steering wheel and kept his eyes nailed to the vast space around them for a bear-shaped shadow that almost certainly wasn't coming. 'If someone calls a false alarm, that's Halloween over for everyone.'

Last time, he'd done this alone—just him and his still dark thoughts. This year, it was kind of nice to have company.

Even if it was thoroughly distracting company.

Her shimmery coat rustled as she turned more fully to him. Even in seats as soft as these ones, sitting still for over an hour was clearly excruciating for a woman who never really *did* still. Kitty reminded him of a shark—as if she stopped swimming, she stopped breathing. Her body, her mind… Just something needed to be busy. Maybe she'd just forgotten how to be still.

'How many jobs do you have up here?' she asked, killing the camera and dropping it to her lap.

'Jobs?'

'Roles,' she clarified. 'How many functions do you fulfil in Churchill?'

'I run land-based search and rescue. That's a twenty-four-seven kind of gig.' Perpetually ready, seldom called on.

'And what else? Apart from helping out at Halloween?'

'I check on the weir daily.' Which she knew. 'And I help out with forest patrols. Sometimes drive special groups around.'

'And you help with bear stuff,' she guessed.

'What makes you say that?'

'Because you know so much for someone who's

only been here two years. And because the locals seem to hold you in some regard.' She narrowed her eyes. 'Even while keeping a careful distance.'

Huh. She made him sound just like one of their bears. And kind of antisocial.

'Are you paid for any of those jobs?' she asked outright.

There was the woman he remembered. Tone deaf. No sense of propriety at all. Just have a thought and act on it. He never did mind that about her. After months of Marcella's careful communication, he'd forgotten how it was to be direct about something.

So he couldn't really complain about it now.

'Manitoba pays me part-time to run the S and R team. That's enough to live on.'

'Pfff. Not at northern prices. I just paid nineteen dollars for four camera batteries.'

Now she wanted to know his expenses? What was she doing? But he'd never been one to shy away from a challenge. So he gave her something without really giving her anything—because he knew that would drive her nuts.

'Don't buy them in tourist season,' was his sage advice. Not surprisingly she didn't appreciate it. 'Why all the interest in my financial status, Kitty?'

Her gaze grew cautious. 'Just wanting to understand how it's all working.'

He thought about letting her off with that. But then he remembered one of his favourite sports five years ago. Baiting the savvy journalist. Testing her mind. Making her do laps.

'That was *what*. Not *why*.'

'I just want...' No one did consternation like Kitty Callaghan. Those little folds right below the dark curls of her fringe only made her more attractive. 'I think I'm trying to make sure you're okay. That you're not struggling.'

Something twisted deep in his gut and the fun sucked right out of this conversation.

'I'm fine. I keep telling you.'

'Well, you would say that, right?'

'You want a doctor's note?'

She puffed a breath into all the tense silence. 'I just want to see it. For myself.'

'Why?'

'Because...' The frown again. She couldn't tell him why she cared—or wouldn't—but when Kitty Callaghan was backed into a corner she just made her own exit. He remembered that about her, too. 'What happened…earlier today…'

Here it came. He should be grateful she'd let it slide this long.

'Was that about Nepal?' she asked.

Lucky he'd had a couple of hours to formulate some kind of easy answer in his head. And he was mostly happy with how casually it came out.

'*That* was about me being frustrated you might have gone and got yourself eaten by wolves. And wondering how I was going to explain that to your employer.'

'My employer wouldn't care as long as my story was filed first,' she snorted, then sobered. 'But what I saw in your eyes wasn't frustration.'

He turned his attention back out to the light field ahead of them and scanned for bears.

His throat felt as if it were full of rubble dust again. 'Can't I just be irritated at how much of my time is being wasted running around after you?'

Kitty's wince made him feel lousier. But she was only here for a few more days. She would go back to her world and he would stay here in his.

And that would be that.

'You've seen a lot of death,' she pushed, bravely. 'You forget what I do for a living?'

'I know that the people you find are usually snap-frozen on some ice face. Or alive. The earth-quakes were very different. That must have been rough.'

It was too exhausting...keeping up hostilities. Besides, while they were talking about strangers under buildings, they weren't talking about Marcella under a tonne of mud. So he relented a little.

'I just brought the dogs to the site,' he played down. 'We did our thing, and as soon as they indicated positive, another team swept in to do the digging and we moved on to a different site.'

Indication after indication after indication.

'Must have been exhausting for them.'

Memories flooded back. *Not just them.*

'Exhaustion is less of a risk than becoming disheartened. The cadaver dogs were indicating every twenty seconds. But the rescue dogs—' the ones trained to find people *alive* '—I had to recruit civilians to go lay in the rubble for them to find. To keep them motivated.'

Her big eyes grew impossibly bigger. 'Will, that's awful.'

He shrugged. 'Too many finds and a cadaver dog becomes traumatised. Too few and a rescue dog stops working. You need to manage them carefully. Give them lots of relief.'

'Is that why you went home to Pokhara? To swap your teams out?'

He sagged back into his leather seats. 'You want details, Kitty? Is that it? Your journalistic mind can't rest until I've painted you a graphic picture of what happened to Marcella?'

'I think *want* is too strong a word,' she said softly. 'But I'd like to understand, yes.'

'The landslide?' he gritted. 'Or me?'

'Both, perhaps. Have you talked about it with anyone?'

He gave her his steeliest glare, the one that he only reserved for really bad behaviour in his dogs. They usually quailed at it. But she didn't, and any moment Kitty's gentle probing was going to poke straight into a nerve cluster.

'*Stop press! Wife buried alive under half a mountain. Man flees from ruins of life.* What's hard to understand about that?'

Most of the blood drained from her face, except two pink splashes where her courage clung stubbornly on.

'Your anger is your grief—'

He raked his fingers through his hair. 'No, Kitty,

my anger is *anger*. I had things all ordered, here. Workable. I had a quiet existence where I could put the past behind me and focus on my work. And now you're determined to drag it all back out into daylight for dissection.'

'I just want to know that you're okay,' she repeated, throwing everything she had left into not allowing the tears he could see brewing behind her eyes to tumble down her pale face.

But he was not about to let himself be moved. 'I'm good.'

'You have no real friends here, Will,' she pointed out. 'No close relationships. That's not okay.'

He chopped the air with an impatient hand. 'You have zero friends and it's a career move. I do it and it's a dysfunction. What's with the double standard?'

'I have friends,' she mumbled.

'None so close that you'd let them know you were okay up here. The only calls you've made were to your office and your parents. Even then you only left a message. Do you truly have no one else who cares for you?'

This time even the pink splashes blanched out. He always had struck back hard.

'Okay,' she relented. 'New subject...'

He splayed a hand and pressed as hard as he could on either side of his skull to dislodge the ache. 'I don't think there are any subjects perky enough to rescue this conversation…'

'Then how about nothing at all? Let's just get through this watch and call it a night. With any luck the airline will have called while we were out…'

Why did that only make him feel more dismal?

He lasted about twenty seconds before the thick silence just about killed him. That same silence that he loved when it swilled around him in his cosy, secure forest cabin. He reached for the door handle.

'You stay put,' he said sternly. 'I'm just going to check in with the perimeter leader.'

And other patently obvious untruths…

The frigid air assaulted his lungs as he left the warmth of the truck cab, but he figured if some little kid could be out in it bound up in origami bed linen then he would survive. Downhill from their position, Churchill was practically aglow with every light in the town illuminated to add to the security and spectacle of this special night. He found himself a convenient patch of shadow between the spill of his own bright headlights and Dom Brennan's, and he tried to dissolve into its darkness, kicking himself for letting Kitty get under his skin.

What did he expect? She was trained to sniff out stories and she had an IQ to rival Einstein's. The two in combination made her well equipped to see through his poorly constructed lies. How long would it be before she started piecing the truth together? She probably had half the story already—Marcella had grabbed onto her like a lifeline when she'd visited, so Kitty probably knew more about his failing relationship with his wife than he did which meant it wouldn't be long before she arrived at the fact that he was responsible for his wife's death.

If he'd been more of a man, he would have packed Marcella up—no matter how she'd protested—and sent her back to the family and life that she'd been trying so very hard not to pine for. If he'd had more courage, he would have pulled the pin on the marriage that had already been flailing eleven months in, and Marcella never would have been in Nepal when the quakes had struck. The hillside house overlooking Pokhara would have been vacant when the earth beneath it had sluiced away.

If he'd had the courage.

He glanced back at the darkened truck. Kitty probably judged him, already, for the thing that had built up between them five years ago—he had been the married one, she hadn't—but did she know just how much of a failure he was as a husband? As a protector? As a basic human being?

Maybe, maybe not. But he certainly wasn't going to start drawing her a roadmap no matter how much she pried.

Not if he could help it.

CHAPTER SIX

THERE WAS NOTHING about the silence of the drive
back to the cabin that was worse than the silence
of the long wait in Will's truck while the trick-or-
treating wound up, but somehow it seemed closer
to Kitty—thicker—without the company of a
dozen other Churchill residents and their trucks
spread out along the ridge overlooking the town.
Or maybe it was just that there was no distraction
to hide behind now.

Kitty turned to him as he drove. 'Listen, Will…'

'What happened to you after Nepal?' he inter-
rupted before she could get her thoughts in a row.
Offence being the best kind of defence and all.
'You were so soaked in passion last time we met.
So in love with life.'

Yes, she had been—with life, with Nepal… And
halfway to falling in love with Will. The first time
she'd ever been totally and utterly at the mercy of
her heart. She'd wandered around the alpine town,
perpetually giddy, half from the oxygen-depleted

air and half from just being around Will. It had been all she could do to channel that emotional energy into other things, more appropriate things.

As if that were going to help.

'Life happened to me,' she hedged, not about to expose herself. 'I grew up.'

'You were twenty-three. And you'd seen more of the world than most people your age.'

I was hardly an adult, either. If she were, wouldn't she have had more sense than to develop feelings for someone else's husband?

She shrugged and hoped it looked more careless than she felt. 'I realised I couldn't waft about for ever, telling any story I liked, living on the hospitality of strangers in every corner of the world. I had to get serious about my career. Build some reserves. Build some prospects.'

'See, that's what I mean.' He threw a frown her way. 'The Kitty Callaghan I knew wouldn't have cared about reserves and prospects.'

Maybe she should have. Then she could have saved herself a tonne of grief.

'You told me you barely knew me,' she reminded him. Back when he'd booted her off his mountainside. 'How would you know what I was then? Or what I am now?'

He must have remembered that conversation, too, because he winced. Did he not like being reminded of the whole sordid *not* affair? Was it just another thing he'd filed away firmly in the past?

'I came home after Nepal, spruced up my résumé and started hunting for stable work.' She counted slowly to three as she eased a breath out. 'The end.'

'Neat coincidence—that your great new life started right after Nepal.'

Air backed up high in her throat and pressed on her heart. There was no way she could answer him with the truth on this one. How hard his comments had hit her. How shamed she'd felt as she'd fled Nepal. For falling for a married man in the first place, for failing to disguise it. For bumbling along like some infatuated teen until he'd had no choice but to send her away. He wasn't responsible for her actions, now or then. But she didn't want to give him that, either. She still had some pride, no matter how dented.

'I'm saying it was my doing. Not yours.'

But the doubt all over his face said otherwise.

She fidgeted with her seat-belt edges. 'Is that what this is about, Will? You're trying to decide how guilty you should feel?'

'I made you feel unwelcome. Like a freeloader.'

Yeah, he had; and a whole bunch of things besides. Some of them terrifyingly new.

Her head filled with the many sideways glances in Nepal as he had worked with his dogs. With the way she'd struggled to keep the feminine tinkle out of her laughter at his tales or the admiration out of her glance as he'd come back in tired and cranky from a long day of training. With the careful distance she'd tried to put between them whenever they had been alone.

With the many times she failed.

Was she doing a better job of hiding it five years on or was he already starting to get twitchy at the signs?

'I'm a big girl, Will. I make my own decisions. I thought it was time to get a bit more serious about my future.'

He dragged his eyes off the road and onto her, long enough, this time, that she began to tighten up inside. But his truck didn't waver. And neither did his gaze. 'I don't like thinking that I…damaged you.'

Her chest ratcheted in another notch. She was not about to give him that. 'I'm hardly broken, Will. I'm just older. As changed as you are.'

He frowned. 'You think I'm changed? How?'

She stared at him. 'You're…flat. Inside.'

She wanted to say 'dead' but it seemed too confronting for him to hear. And despite the hurt Will had caused her in the past, she wasn't interested in returning the favour. Not intentionally.

But how much could she say without saying too much?

'What you do for a living is amazing. In Nepal, I watched you working that mountain and was blown away by your courage and focus. Your natural intelligence. Your gift with the dogs. None of that has changed on the surface but there was something…deeper…underlying all of that and it's gone now. It's like your faith in the world has vanished. Like you're just going through the motions. And I understand why that might be, but it used to light you up from the inside and make all those other aspects more pronounced. That's what's changed.'

His eyes slashed sideways, but the lurch of his Adam's apple took the sting out of the graze.

'You're strong for everyone all the time. I just wanted to be there for you now so that you could let that go for a few minutes. So I could carry all the weight for you. I wasn't quizzing you for the sake of it or to snoop. I'd like to think that I could put a friend's well-being above my professional curiosity.'

'We're friends, are we?' he gritted.

Thump, thump, thump... 'You tell me.'

He glowered at her in the shadows of the darkened cab and she thought he was going to let the silence answer for him. But then he spoke, to make it perfectly clear.

'I honestly don't think we can be, Kitty.'

Her guts flipped back on themselves and twisted into a knot that choked. 'Why not?'

He pulled to the side of the empty road and the inertia swayed her in her seat. The truck's headlights slashed out into the dark, dark forest ahead. He turned to her and gave her his full attention.

If she weren't so angry she'd have thought about how alone they were. How close...

'Because it hasn't gone away. That thing between us. If we're being honest.'

Shock stole her breath—and then shock pawned it in some dingy back-alley store never to be recovered—but somehow she managed to squeeze a few words out without a break in her voice.

'What *thing*?'

But far more notably: *Between* us?

He just stared at her, daring her to continue denying it. But she wasn't about to expose herself like that. Not to him. If he wasn't interested in being friends, fine, but she wasn't going to do his dirty work for him. She sat up straighter and met his eyes head-on. 'What thing, Will?'

Because he'd made it clear five years ago that *her* feelings were the reason she couldn't stay.

But the longer he sat there in silence, staring, the clearer it all became. And the clearer it became, the more heat burbled up around her until it just had to come spurting out of the only available opening.

'Are you serious?' she hissed like the pressure cooker she was.

'You're angry?'

'Five years, Will! You've let me think that throwing me off your mountain was all about me developing a thing for you. That it was my own fault.'

Five years!

He frowned. 'I never said it was just you—'

'You never said it wasn't!'

And then, a heartbeat behind that, a tiny voice whispered in her heart and did a joyous little backflip.

It wasn't?

'Why would I send you away if it was just *your* feelings at stake?' he defended weakly. 'I would have just distanced myself.'

No... No! He didn't get to make this her fault, too. 'You said you loved Marcella—'

'I did love her.'

'—and then you sent me away.'

Oh, wasn't this fun? Reliving it together. But it felt so much better doing it angry. There was no room for sorrow while she was this worked up.

He dropped his eyes. 'I know.'

'And at no time anywhere in there did you happen to mention that the attraction was mutual!'

Confusion twisted his features. 'I assumed it was obvious.'

'No,' she gritted. 'It was not obvious.'

Because if she had known, she would have left long before being asked.

He stared at her in the half-glassy way that told her he was replaying the whole miserable incident from her point of view. And that meant she was witnessing the exact moment he realised what she'd believed all this time. What he'd sent her off that mountain believing.

'Damn, Kitty—'

'I cannot believe you!'

'That was a hard conversation for me, too,' he defended. 'I didn't exactly rehearse it.'

'Five years, Will!'

He took a deep breath, studied his white knuckles on the steering wheel for a bit and then came back to her. 'Okay. I get it. I might not have been fully explicit—'

She choked on the umbrage.

'—but the fact remains that was why you couldn't stay. Because I loved my wife and we were having a tough time. I couldn't develop feelings for you, let alone trust them.'

Her outrage started to wane as empathy took hold. But she didn't let it go without a fight.

'Having a tough time, how?' Though what her heart was screaming was, *What kind of feelings?*

To buy himself some time, Will pushed the truck into gear and moved off slowly. It was the vehicular equivalent of nervously clearing his throat. Kitty sagged back into her seat, waited. She would wait another five years if it meant putting Nepal behind her once and for all.

It took him nearly that long to reply.

'What did Marcella tell you about her background?' he asked as he negotiated the turn-off to his cabin.

The change of tack threw her momentarily but she dragged her focus along on the tangent. 'I know she was from Louisiana. Big family. I know her family wanted her to teach but she wanted to paint. That's about it.'

'Did you know they didn't want us to marry?'

It was surreal, talking about this so dispassionately. As though she weren't still harbouring her feelings for Will—or a facsimile of them.

'No. I didn't.'

'They wanted Marcella to go to a theological college. Really, I think they would have been happiest if she'd just got on with the job of having a family. Like her sisters. They rode her pretty hard.'

'Shouldn't they have been excited about you two marrying, then?'

'Not when they discovered I was going to Nepal. But that only made me more attractive to Marcella. She redoubled her efforts, then.'

Her efforts?

Kitty blinked. 'You think she married you to get away from her family's influence?'

He glanced at her after he took the corner. 'I know she did.'

'The woman I met adored you.'

'I believe she wanted to. But mostly I think I was just a convenient ticket out of Louisiana to a life she could forge for herself. A way to be free and just paint.'

Deep sadness washed past his eyes. Her freedom wasn't that long-lived, in the end.

'Turns out Marcella didn't know herself as well as her family did, and I sure didn't. At first, she loved the light and the scenery and the excitement of the bohemian lifestyle, but it wasn't long before she stopped painting. Stopped going down into Pokhara city to explore. She struggled in Nepal, almost from the start. Found the culture confusing, the diet too different, the mountains oppressive.'

The majestic Annapurnas? She'd found them so inspiring, herself. So incredibly wild.

'About the only thing she related to was the faith; the Nepalese were about as gentle as she was. But I was just getting established and so my work called me away from home a lot, kept me busy. Took me from her when she needed me.'

The woman she'd met started to reframe in her

mind. All that midnight roaming, all those fragile smiles. All the wine… Will was assuming responsibility for that. Or maybe he'd always assumed it.

'Deep down I knew why she married me. But I went ahead with it because I saw so much potential for the person she was going to blossom into away from her family. I thought one of us would be enough to start with.'

'It wasn't?'

He pulled into his drive and killed the engine, then sat staring out into the darkness around his property.

'Five years ago Marcella was at her lowest ebb. I'd retreated into my work and she was grasping at any displacement activity to distract her from the reality of the life she'd chosen.'

'And then I arrived,' Kitty realised.

'You saw her at her best,' he acknowledged. 'Having you there was like having one of her sisters there and she perked right up. She was infected by your light and sunshine and even, a little bit, by your love of the place. She saw Nepal differently through your eyes. But when you left she slid right back again.'

He turned in his seat. 'That's why I asked you to go, Kitty. Because it was the lowest moment in our marriage and because having you there reminding me of what was possible was just too dangerous.'

Dangerous. Not difficult, not hard.

Dangerous.

Something twisted around her lungs, slowly constricting.

'I should have found a way to tell you that I was sending you away because of my feelings, not yours. I'm sorry.'

Five years was still five years, but somehow she couldn't find it in herself to be angry in the face of his sorrow. Still, the thumping in her chest threatened to swell up and block her airway.

'What feelings?'

Blue ice glanced up. 'Do you remember our conversations? Do you remember the laughter, Kitty? The connection?'

Half of her was frustrated that he was avoiding the question. The other half of her was still thrilling that they were having this discussion at all.

'Yes,' she breathed.

'Did you miss it, ever?'

Every day.

'Yes.'

He just nodded. As if to say 'me too'.

'That's why I think we can't be friends. Because that's there. Still there.'

If anything was going to stop her being Will's friend it was the memory of that last day. Turned out she wanted to be that friend more than she feared it.

'Guess I'm just more of an optimist,' she said, simply.

The mood in the truck thawed. It wasn't charged, it was just…clear. He tipped his bent head up to her.

'How much of that Zurich story do you still have to cut?' he asked.

She sank back into the passenger seat as if it were a sofa. 'All of it. Someone interrupted my audio recording.'

How could a smile change so essentially from one moment to the next? Somehow, this one was full of olive branch and acceptance. 'Can you do a bunch of editing tonight, make some headway?'

'Probably.' Definitely. She was going to need a good clear space from Will to process everything he'd just said. 'Why?'

'Because I'm doing a favour for someone tomorrow morning, bussing a bunch of science teachers out to the research centre. Will probably take most of the morning but I can show you the conservation zone while we're out there. Maybe see some wild bears doing their thing, more to your satisfaction.'

She grinned at him from her comfortable nook in the darkness. 'If their *thing* isn't tap dancing, I'm going to be very disappointed.'

'Up to you. You're welcome to tag along. Properly welcome,' he added when she lifted a questioning brow.

'If I get a call from the airport...?'

The ticking clock intruded as surely as if she'd wound down her window; it sucked all the warmth from inside the vehicle. Had they both forgotten that the moment her flight came up she was off, back to her busy, busy life far from here?

'Leave it in the hands of fate,' he murmured, levering his door handle. 'I leave here at seven-thirty. With or without you.'

CHAPTER SEVEN

'GOOD NEWS!' THE WOMAN from the airline said down the phone early the following morning when Kitty called to check on the status of her repatriation. 'Your airline has made the necessary arrangements with the local airline to start getting you all home.'

The emotion Kitty felt at that news wasn't quite the rush of relief she expected. Instead it was a slow, seeping disappointment. But she wasn't entirely sure what she was so disenchanted about. Missing out on some sightseeing?

Or missing out on something more?

'But…we have quite a backlog of passengers to clear,' the woman went on. 'I don't have you on either of today's flights, I'm sorry. Tomorrow perhaps.'

Perhaps? 'Are you serious?'

'It's bear season, ma'am, and we have one hundred and sixty people to re-seat on flights that are already full with paying customers. We're re-seating by original seat number.'

Which meant the passengers in First and Business Class would be shipped out first and then they'd start chewing their way through good old cattle class. Kitty's sense of social justice reared up and bellowed over the disappointment of just moments before.

'I *am* a paying customer,' she reminded the airport official, even though she was handing her a legitimate opportunity to stay longer in Churchill. Which meant staying longer with Will.

'We're doing our best, ma'am.'

If she said *ma'am* one more time… She was twenty-eight, not seventy-eight.

'Okay,' Kitty sighed into the phone. 'Just keep me informed. Thank you.'

She lowered the handset on Will's portable phone then went hunting for its charging station just for something to do. To walk off a little of the irritation. Of course they had to have a system; it would be chaos if they were just randomly issuing whatever seats they had available. And of course they had to get the people who'd paid a year's wage for their seats out first even if they weren't the kind of people who were even on wages.

Unlike her.

Her income was directly linked to her ability to file stories. Her programme director had tersely accepted that her being stranded was outside her control. He'd ordered Kitty to stream her raw vision to their Shanghai headquarters so someone else could cut it. But she'd be damned if she'd let someone else cut her story. Or submit it. Or steal it.

Especially if that someone was Mei.

Features on CNTV's Sunday morning business programme were way too hard to secure.

So she would quietly ignore her director's request as long as she could and cut the story herself, here, then stream the finished piece to Shanghai. Less data cost for Will. More control for her.

But all of that could wait. She had places to be and bears to see…

'Looks like you've got company,' she called down the hall as she gathered up her things.

There was a longish pause before Will answered and she briefly wondered if he'd changed his mind. Just because things between them had thawed a little last night…

Thawed a lot. Somewhere in her five-year history with Will she had assigned him Superman status—maybe because of what he did for a living, maybe because of some intrinsically capable quality of his own—but every Superman had a mortal side and, last night, Will had shown her his Clark Kent.

For a moment.

'All right. Bring your camera,' he called.

She glanced at her open suitcase where she had a digital SLR, a pocket camera, a high-def video camera. And of course her phone. 'Which one?' she yelled.

In the end, she brought all of them, causing Will to roll his eyes as she bundled towards his truck.

'Lucky we're not hiking,' he muttered.

She glanced at him as he moved around to the other side of the vehicle. The scrappy beard was gone. 'Did you shave?'

'Nope.'

That's what you get for asking a dumb question.

They stopped in at the weir to do the morning check and raise the flag, after which it took just fifteen minutes to get into town and pick up the bus and keys from Will's associate, Travis.

'My eldest is getting his wisdom teeth yanked, today,' Travis explained. 'Otherwise I'd be doing this run myself. I'll go back for the group this afternoon.'

She glanced at Will. 'We're leaving tourists alone out in the tundra?'

Pfff. Two days in town and she was declassifying herself as a tourist?

'Sure,' Will said. 'They wanted a true northern experience.'

He went about loading her gear onto the front seat of the bus, right behind the driver's seat. The first thing she saw as she climbed up into the bus behind him was the shotgun subtly tucked in next to it.

'Really?' she asked, distracted by the firearm.

He stopped and turned. 'No, Kit. Not really. They're teachers, not survivalists. We're dropping them at the remote research centre where they have a full, fully supervised day programme waiting for them. On the way back you and I will detour and see if we can spot any bears.'

Heat rushed up her neck.

For a woman so close to thirty, she sure spent a lot of time flushing around Will.

'Having a bus licence one of your many talents?' she asked, to move the focus off her new super power—gullibility.

He paused before answering and she wondered if he was thinking about the best answer. Or the safest. 'It's not far. And these are quiet roads.'

She caught herself just as she was lowering herself into the seat closest to the doors. 'You're unlicensed for large vehicles. Are you kidding?'

'There's a good chance Trav is probably unlicensed and he owns the bus.' He grinned. 'Stuff like that is a bit more…negotiable up here. If you *can* drive a bus safely then you can drive a bus in Churchill.'

Turned out Will *could* drive a bus. He navigated the luxury people mover easily out of town and pulled up at the front of the airport where thirty science types climbed on fresh off their just-landed flight. They came from all over Canada, up to study different aspects of the subarctic biome, and this was just the first of several visits they were planning on making out to the research centre. They'd lost one day of their research trip to the same ice rain holding her hostage but they'd lost none of their enthusiasm. Within minutes, the bus filled with excited science-speak. And *passion*. So much of it. The bus was awash with people who loved what they did for a living and knew they were making a difference. Kitty sat back and just soaked it all in, glancing now and again at Will, who was taking the roads very seriously.

I remember this.

This was her: fresh out of uni with a double major in Journalism and Media when she'd thought she was going to solve the problems of the world—or at least expose them to great fanfare and critical acclaim. Lord, that had been a lifetime ago. Now she worked for a cashed-up corporate network in China and produced stories about rich people for even richer people.

And she couldn't remember the last time she'd got an excited flush going to work. Even flying somewhere new had grown tiresome.

The roads might have been as quiet as Will had promised, but it was still a forty-minute drive out to the research centre, picking their way through the tundra, all those teacher noses pressed to the glass to get their first glimpse of the natural habitat. Up close, tundra wasn't flat at all; it was pocked with lakes and swamps, with causeways of passable sedges only where the permafrost below had pushed the ground up into ridges. And it wasn't solid, either; a sparsely treed, waterlogged moor littered with enormous boulders dumped there by a prehistoric glacier and with a thin crunch of seasonal ice starting to form.

Behind her, the group's leader chatted to the others about 'isostatic rebound' and 'Goldilocks Zones' and they all nodded and took notes and generally grew more and more fascinated as they whizzed by all that view.

'The flora up here only has between fifty and one hundred frost-free days to grow,' the man said, 'which of course informs the diversity.'

Of course it did...

Kitty caught Will's eyebrow lift in the rear-view mirror. 'Learning stuff?'

She faked taking notes onto her hand, and muttered under her breath. 'Informing...the...diversity...'

He chuckled and went back to getting his passengers safely to the research centre. It was a massive building designed to sit naturally in the landscape while also managing to stand out architecturally. She'd expected it to be out in the middle of nowhere—and it was—but it wasn't out there alone. It was sited on an old, ramshackle airforce base.

'Officially, the Canadian military were studying the aurora out here during the fifties,' he told her as the thirty passengers all filed off, offering him their cheery thanks. 'With rockets.'

Officially? 'You don't think so?'

'Check it out on a globe and not a flat map. Straight over the top of the planet, it's a very short distance to Russia as the crow flies.'

Or as the missile does. Her journalist's curiosity was immediately piqued. The image of two superpowers with stockpiles of missiles all pointed at each other—*just in case.*

'There we go.' Will grinned. 'That's what I've been waiting for.'

She brought her focus back to him. 'What?'

His fingers brushed the creases between her brows and her skin leapt at the gentle touch. Was that the first time that he'd ever touched her intentionally? Almost intimately?

Her heartbeat certainly thought so.

'That spark of imagination,' he said. 'The intrigue. I've missed that.'

'You don't think the Zurich story sparks my imagination?'

The look he gave her said *no.* Clearly. 'You don't look like that when you talk about it.'

'CNTV's viewers are hardly going to be excited by a seventy-year-old, speculative *what if*,' she said.

'I don't much care what excites them. I'm more interested in what excites you.'

He didn't mean that. Not the way her deviant mind suddenly went. But the very idea that Will Margrave would give any thought at all to her excitement levels…

Her throat tightened right up.

'Didn't you promise me bears?' she squeezed, sinking back into her seat to put some much-needed distance between them. And to dislodge the delicious tension suddenly stretching between them.

They left the research centre and its decaying military neighbour and headed back towards the shore. The journey was more tranquil without the energetic hubbub of thirty science teachers but it was also less educative. Kitty made herself happy just soaking up the view out of the bus's massive front windows. At least one of those views had Will in it, seated at the wheel of this big vehicle, shotgun by his thigh. Commanding. Masculine. Utterly cowboy-esque. The sort of view she never would have let herself enjoy in the past but now would hold close to her heart for ever.

You're checking out the bus driver, a tiny voice admonished and she had to turn her chuckle away to the passing landscape.

They bumped back on asphalt then travelled parallel with the vast Hudson Bay coast until Will called back to her. 'The conservation zone is right ahead, but we're not licensed to go in there, so we're going to lurk on its fringes.'

'Huh… So there's some licences you *do* care about,' she replied. 'Good to know.'

He gave her a look that was almost as eloquent as flipping her the bird. But when he spoke all he said was, 'You might want to lower a few windows for your photos.'

Open window. Wild animals… 'Is that safe?'

Blue eyes flicked to her in the mirror. Saving people was his life's work; he wasn't about to risk someone carelessly. Even her.

Right.

'Only the small top ones drop. You'll have plenty of time to put them up again. There's not going to be a bear stampede when we get there.'

Minutes later, Will pulled the bus to a halt and checked the full perimeter before turning back to her. 'Want to open that gate for me?'

She followed his gaze out of the front window

to the massive swing gate with the faded 'Private Property' sign dangling on it. Then she brought them back to him. 'You're kidding, right?'

He smiled. 'Then close it right up after I've driven through.'

She thought about protesting that it wasn't his land, or that she'd be eaten by a bear, or that he should get his bus licence before being authorised to order someone to get off one amidst wild animals, but then it occurred to her that this was a test.

Will was testing her. And, in Will, a test was almost as good as flirting. It was how he let you know he was there.

And she never failed tests. Ever.

On principle.

'Fine.'

She slung her legs free of the plush seat and descended the three front steps down onto terra firma when Will opened the folding doors. She wanted to be cool; she wanted to just leap off, open the gate and close it again afterwards without so much as a glance around her. But this was bear country and, while she absolutely trusted Will, she didn't trust the bears. So she couldn't help glancing around her anxiously as she hurried to pull the gate wide and then close it again when he was through.

'Reminds you you're alive, doesn't it?' He laughed as she scampered back on, puffing.

She sagged back into her seat as the pneumatic doors closed them safely in. But, yeah, it really did. Her pulse was up, her blood was flowing and she had just enough adrenaline still whipping through it to heighten her senses. Already the place where the tundra met the deep grey waters of the bay was looking brighter and more magical.

'You're going to tell me there's no bears for miles, aren't you?'

His laugh burst through the empty bus. 'Not *miles...*'

He trundled the bus about that far at a reasonable pace before he slowed and started scanning the horizon. Then he just quietly positioned the bus and killed the engine. Kitty couldn't help craning her neck. Then standing. Then walking the full length of the empty bus, scanning three hundred and sixty degrees all around them. The snow-dusted tundra stretched all the way to the horizon on two sides, and it fell away to Hudson Bay in front. This must have been the limit of that terra-forming glacier because it seemed to have bulldozed a mountain of worn, round boulders here. Most as big as the bus that was keeping them safe. Nothing more than cake sprinkles to the power of glacial ice.

'To your right,' Will said quietly.

No, she'd just looked right, but she followed his finger and sure enough…

Just like the one at the weir, this polar bear was doing a whole lot of nothing. Vast amounts of nothing, in fact. It was stretched out on a couple of flat, low rocks that weren't yet completely buried in snow, sun-baking. Except that there was no sun visible through the clouds. And no heat to bake in. Was ice-baking a thing? Kitty rushed to get her cameras out, but the bear didn't move an inch, making her scrambling unnecessary.

'I was looking for something yellower,' she justified as she lined up her shot. This bear looked as white as the snow around it.

'Transparent hair follicles,' Will said as she fiddled with her exposure settings. 'We just see it as white. It's still the same colour.'

She turned and stared at him while his attention was fully on the bear.

'Bear, Kitty,' he said softly, without taking his eyes off the horizon.

Right...

Her longest lenses got her nice and close. She fired off dozens of urgent shots before realising the bear truly was not moving. Nor planning to, it seemed. Blinking, yes, but not about to come barrelling at them like something from the natural history films she'd studied at university.

'And over in the willow on your left,' Will murmured. Not because the bear might hear him but just because it was the kind of moment that demanded whispering.

The second bear stretched up from its sleeping place in the willow sticks and stuck its nose in the air to breathe them in. They must have smelled vaguely interesting because it hauled itself out and onto all fours before wandering in their general direction. Without the stretch, she never would have seen it in there. A person could walk right past and not know it was there.

The thought was sobering.

The willow bear lumbered ever closer as her camera whizzed, but at the last minute it changed trajectory and lazily wandered over to the rock bear and nudged it with its snout before sitting down hard on its big bottom, sending up a puff of snow.

Kitty wondered if there was smoke coming from her camera at the rate she was taking pictures.

'That's a play entreaty,' Will said from somewhere behind her. She hadn't noticed him move. 'Get ready...'

Rock bear seemed entirely uninterested in any gestures from its friend, turning away to peer out to sea. But—just as Kitty lowered her camera—it reared up into sitting position and then straight up onto its back feet with an open-mouthed roar. On four legs, it had to be five feet tall; on two legs, it was a giant. Heart hammering, Kitty thrust her still camera back to Will, who had moved in behind her, and she scrabbled for her video as the bears began to tussle and lunge at each other, twisting and surging in combat and sending snow dust flying. Through the lens of her video camera, their massive canine teeth glinted against the northern sun as they showed them off for each other. But the bears weren't in any hurry and they weren't terribly serious; having woken from their respective naps, they were more interested in playing...and playing...and playing.

'How long could this go for?' Kitty finally asked Will as the bears continued their mock battle, this time back on all fours, advancing and retreating like an ursine tango.

'Until they get tired.'

'Shouldn't they be conserving their energy?'

The loose skin under their thick coats swung as they scrapped with each other. Kitty tried to imagine what they would be like all padded out with a tonne of seal fat.

'I think they know the ice isn't far away, so perfecting their fighting skills is more important than preserving the last remnants of body fat they have left. They have to get ready.'

She turned to look back at him. 'For what?'

'The real deal. The bears out on the tundra are mostly males; they're friendly now but when the ice comes they'll have to fight for feeding grounds and for access to females. The battles won't be so gentle then.'

The thought of those beautiful coats streaked with blood...

'I'm trying to imagine them battling over a female...'

'It's worth it,' he said from behind her. 'For the right woman.'

Her chest squeezed until she reminded it that he was talking about Marcella. His loyalty heartened and hurt to the same degree. That she would never know that kind of love…

Kitty let her camera sag. But the spectacle was too great as the willow bear began to chase the rock bear.

'This will look so good in slow motion,' she mumbled to herself, zooming in to capture more of the run.

With no warning, her lens was blocked by a massive pink palm as Will stretched his hand around her from behind and lowered the camera until all she was filming was the bus floor.

'You're missing all the action,' he admonished, close to her ear.

She twisted her camera free of his hand, but didn't move out from within the warm circle of his body. His breath against her ear caused an avalanche of tingles.

'I am now…' she muttered, irritated at the instant response from her undisciplined flesh.

But he wasn't going to be deterred. 'Just watch, Kit. Record it in your memory instead. This could be the only time you see it.'

Will might as well have asked her to step off the bus and go out to join the game of bear chase; if he did it in that breathy voice, that close to her ear, she would say yes to just about anything. She lowered her camera to the upholstered bus seat and tucked it safely into the crease. Then she lifted her gaze and just watched, half mesmerised by the nature show, half mesmerised by the heat-soak of Will's body so close to hers.

As rapidly as it started, the chase was off, and the willow bear plonked down exactly where it stopped and turned to consider the world. Instantly deep in bear thoughts. The massive rock bear slowed its jog first to a lope and then to a gentle stroll. But its blood—and its curiosity—were up now and it turned its massive head in their direction. Kitty moved to close her window.

'Look at the size of him, Kit...'

He was right. That bear wasn't getting through that small top window any time soon.

She leaned forward as the bear approached the side of the bus and disappeared below the view of the windows. Pressed against the glass, she could just see him sniffing around the bus's wheels.

'He's nibbling the tyre!'

Will stretched over the top of her to monitor the bear, too. 'A nibble's fine as long as he doesn't sink those canines in.'

The thought of having to be rescued from the

tundra in an incapacitated bus was almost as un-appealing as trying to change its tyre with two bears passing her the tools.

Rock bear wandered the length of the bus, peering up at the windows curiously. Kitty was tempted to follow it along the aisle, but her view pressed against the window was probably better anyway. At the rear of the bus, the bear pressed back up onto two feet and wobbled there, precariously, peering in through the tinted windows of the bus.

'Oh, Will…!'

Immediately after she made the sound, it turned and pinned her with its gaze. It plonked back to Earth and strolled directly to her row in the bus where it paused—for a bear heartbeat—before pushing once again to its back legs and ducking its head to peer through her open window. It found her eyes and locked onto them hard with its small dark ones.

All breath caught in her throat instinctively at the massive size and proximity of the hungry predator.

Vaguely she was aware of Will's hands closing around her shoulders and slowly easing her back from the window as the bear twisted its big head right in through the opening.

'Easy, now…' Will crooned in that sure, velvet tone he had. Whether his words were intended for the bear or for her, it didn't matter. They helped to ease her racing heart, just the same.

The bear stretched its curious head forwards, sniffing the air and gazing around the bus's interior. Up this close it was far more teddy-like than a dangerous animal had a right to be, its small fortune-cookie ears, broad brow and wide-set eyes set in damp, golden fur. By far its most dominant feature was the enormous wet black nose, which it pressed as far forward as its thick neck would allow through the narrow window.

Close enough to touch.

The puff of its hot, stale breath made the loose hairs around her face dance.

It seemed incongruous that such a massive animal should make such a thin, sharp whine, and it took a moment for Kitty to realise that it was coming from deep in her own throat.

'Shh…'

Will eased her back into his body and crossed strong arms across her chest—as if that would keep her safe against the bear should it have a brain snap and surge right through the glass. But it didn't, of course it didn't. One look at the bear and Kitty could tell it was simply curious about this new arrival in its otherwise empty day. Not to say that it wouldn't have shown any interest had they happened to have pockets full of bacon, but this bear wasn't interested in eating either of them. It just wanted to look.

As she had the thought, the bear drew his big head back out of the upper window and stretched up more fully to peer over the roof of the bus, pressing its dinner-plate paws against the glass for balance. Even standing down on the ground, his shoulders were higher than Kitty's standing up high in the bus. Extended like this, he truly dwarfed them.

And then he was gone. Back to the ground, back to his friend from the willow. Back to his ice-baking.

Kitty sagged into Will, struggling to catch breath that had grown choppy and to master the thick clog of tears that seemed to be frozen—just as she was—deep in her chest somewhere.

'What do you think of our savage predators now?' he murmured against her ear.

Her answer was more croak than speech. Will

leaned past her, kneeling amongst her camera gear on the seat to slide the small window back up into locked position, and then returned both his feet to the ground, turning her in the circle of his arms.

'Wow,' she croaked, peering up at him wide-eyed.

'Glad you came?'

Glad was way too tame for the emotions she was feeling. Somewhere deep down she wished she were being much cooler in this moment—or at least more loquacious—but single syllables seemed to be her limit while her body was still reacting instinctually to the presence of such an arch predator.

Slowly—so slowly—she became aware of things around her again. The growing warmth of the bus's air now that the window was closed. The shotgun now propped within easy reach on the seat next to them. The closeness of Will's body against hers.

She fluttered her fingers up to touch her bear-blown hair.

'So close...'

Okay, two syllables were better than one. She was getting there.

Will's fingers joined hers to help put her hair to

rights. Each one started a riot in her flesh where they brushed. 'He just wanted to say hi.'

Will's smile radiated the heat she needed to unfreeze her speech cortex. She peered up at him as if it were the first time she'd seen him. And—totally of their own accord—the fingers of her right hand reached up to lie against his cheek.

'You did shave.'

Three words. Excellent progress.

His laugh took him a pace away from her and, once achieved, he seemed to remember the sense of that. Which only served to highlight how eager she was for him not to do it. He rubbed her upper arms firmly and restored some sense with the blood flow.

'I feel like I'm drunk,' she wobbled.

'It's the adrenaline,' he said. 'Here, get some of this into you.'

He produced a thermos of coffee from somewhere and poured her a liberal dose into the cupped lid. Then she sagged down amongst her camera gear and sipped it while watching the two bears continue to interact out on the tundra. After an eternity—and a second coffee—the two parted ways and one wandered back to its willow bed.

'I had them all wrong,' she breathed, warmer now inside and out.

'They're dangerous because of their size and because they're unused to being around people, but they're not more of a killer than the foxes they share the tundra with. Or the seals they eat.'

'His paws on the window. Like dinner plates.'

'They're big animals.' She knew when she was being humoured but, right now, humouring was what she needed. In the absence of stroking.

'I just wanted to touch it…' She frowned, re-membering.

Will laughed. 'I know. I was there. That wouldn't have been a good idea.'

The image started to come back to her and she chuckled. 'It was like I was hypnotised.'

'You resisted, that's what counts.'

'You had to restrain me,' she pointed out.

That seemed to remind them both of how closely they'd stood, Will's arms crossed across her soft body, pulling her back into his hard one.

She studied the empty cup in her hands, then brought her face back up. 'Thank you, Will. Truly. I will never forget this day.'

He relieved her of the empty thermos lid, his brush lingering on her fingers as he did. 'You're welcome. Maybe we'll get another chance to see them.'

We. Not you.

Old habits—the desire to protect herself—made her shrug. 'If not for the fact that the airline started flying people out today.'

Which meant she could be leaving as soon as tomorrow.

Confusion chased the disappointment across his strong jaw just as the two bears had lumbered across the whitened tundra. And he took a step back. 'Well, then, you'll always have your first bear.'

He returned the shotgun to its place by the driver's seat and Kitty took her cue. It took only moments to return all but one camera to her equipment bag.

'So whose land are we trespassing on?' she asked brightly, to do her bit in putting things back on a safer footing.

He took his time fitting the thermos back into its holder. 'Relax, it's mine.'

She turned and stared. 'What?'

'Marcella's life insurance,' he began, awkwardly. 'It was enough to buy this land. In her name.'

Kitty peered back out at the stunning, bear-littered tundra.

'It was a way to preserve it for the wildlife for ever. Against any future development. The great-great-great-grandcubs of those bears will still be resting there in a hundred years, thanks to her.'

Tears rushed in and made blinking them back impossible. So she swiped at them instead.

'Does that upset you?' he asked.

She tried to reply and found that she could not. Marcella was making a difference even from beyond the grave. That simple truth hurt her in ways that Will could not possibly imagine. She'd never felt more inadequate than at this moment. Because what kind of a difference was she making...?

'I think it's beautiful,' Kitty finally squeezed out, heart aching. 'The perfect thing. She would have loved painting this.'

'Yeah,' he agreed, his own voice not quite steady.

He keyed the bus up to rumbling, giving the distant rock bear cause to lift his big head and see them off, and effectively ending the conversation. Kitty sank back into her seat and stared out of the window at Marcella's land.

So beautiful and fragile... As she had been.

As if bears weren't exciting enough for one day, she saw through the window something else that she hadn't yet seen in Churchill. It was only a glimpse, but it was there.

'Blue sky!' she called up to Will.

He followed her glance and willingly grabbed the change in conversation. 'Yep. The ceiling is officially lifting. If your luck holds you might even get a hint of aurora before you leave.'

She knew the eyes she turned up to him would be as big as bear paws. It would be hard to top today's beautiful experience but the Northern Lights—proper lights, in the actual north—would come close.

Bears. The aurora borealis.

And an opportunity to hang out with a thawing Will Margrave...

As disasters went, this unexpected layover in Churchill was working out better than she'd imagined.

CHAPTER EIGHT

CNTV's SHANGHAI OFFICE picked up after three rings and she wondered which of three senior producers was doing the graveyard shift. A woman barked into the receiver, long distance.

Kitty's eyelids squeezed closed. 'Evening, Mei-Xiu...'

Her Wicked Step-Colleague.

'Kitty? Where the hell is your story?' her producer said in clipped English.

Hello, Kitty, how are you? I heard you had an emergency landing in the sub-arctic. Hope you're okay...

'Did you get the voiceover track I filed?' Kitty cut in. 'And the script?'

'Wen-Hau was looking at it today,' Mei snipped. 'But it's not much to work with. I need the raw vision.'

Yeah she did—if Mei wanted to file the story herself.

'I was up all night cutting it,' Kitty stressed,

down the line. And not sending the vision until it was fully cut was the only way she would keep control of the story. 'I'll get it to you tomorrow.'

'Oh, sure,' Mei-Xiu quipped and Kitty had no trouble imagining her perfectly made-up face turning ugly. 'Tomorrow, the next day. What's the rush? It's just the Sunday feature.'

'I'm still in Churchill,' Kitty said, extra loud to compensate for the long distance. 'I'm wait-listed but—'

Mei's reply could have stripped paint. She had quite the grasp of English colloquialisms when she wanted to. 'Do you know how many corre-spondents would kill for that feature spot?'

Yes. Intimately. She'd been them for so long.

'Tomorrow,' she promised, though her heart wasn't in it.

Mei scowled. It saturated her voice. 'Arctic to-morrow or Chinese tomorrow?'

Right... Because it was already tomorrow in Shanghai. That invisible clock that constantly ticked in Kitty's ears kicked up a notch. Maybe she should call the airport back... But no, she could edit this story much better from here than she could sitting in a crowded airport with insuf-ficient Wi-Fi to go around.

'I'm on it, Mei. Trust me.'

Yeah. That wasn't going to happen. Nobody trusted anyone else in their game. Right now she was threatening to make Mei-Xiu look bad to the programme director and Mei wasn't going to take that sitting down. She'd climbed about as high as she was ever going to and younger, shinier performers were coming up under her all the time. Mei was desperate enough to bin any story she did send and just say she never received it.

'You file by Thursday or I file something for you.'

The phone went dead.

Goodbye to you, too…

Kitty flopped back onto her bed, exhausted already, and stared sideways out of the massive picture window. Out back, the dark trees were dusted with snow that hadn't quite managed to thaw out from overnight. So pretty… It was tempting just to lose herself in that picturesque vista rather than apply herself to a story she was rapidly losing heart for.

She rolled over and reached for her laptop, which had the first five and a half minutes of her eight-minute feature already cut from last night's editing session. Will had left her to it on getting back from the bus trip—he'd been a little bit too relieved, she'd thought—and busied himself elsewhere. He'd even brought her the thermos so she didn't have to emerge to refresh her coffee.

Kind, if not for her sneaking suspicion that he wanted to force some personal space.

Five years hadn't done anything to diminish the energy between them yesterday morning. The way his voice caressed the hairs on the back of her neck. The way the heat of his skin reached out across all this cold and brushed against her. The way her head rushed simply from standing near him—in a way that had nothing to do with all the extra oxygen in the air. It was as thrilling as it was distracting. But none of it meant that Will was necessarily interested in starting up where they'd never left off. Judging by the way he'd arranged things so she barely needed to poke her head out of the room all day, then conveniently had business last night, maybe he was already in damage-control mode. So the best she could hope for from this unexpected stranding on the sub-arctic isle of Margrave was that they might end up slightly better friends than they'd managed before.

Still, when you had fewer actual friends than

you could count on the fingers on one hand, that was no small achievement.

Her laptop beeped at her as it prepared to drop into power-saver mode and she snapped back to the present and refocused on her day's edit and the pull shot from one of Zurich's medieval church spires to the ultra-modern Prime Tower. It might not fill her with the kind of excitement that tussling bears did—not even remotely—but, right now, her relationship with her career was the only one she should be focusing on.

Because success wasn't going to make itself.

Will stood over Kitty as she slept, sprawled out across her bed, a half-eaten apple still in her hand.

'Kitty?' Nothing. She didn't even twitch.

Wow, she really slept like the dead. Just how late had she worked? He swapped his torch to his left hand and placed the right gently on her shoulder, feeling like an intruder all the while.

'Kitty? Come on, wake up.'

He wanted to feel closer to her, the kind of close that meant it was okay to slide his hand across her shoulder and brush her cheek to wake her more gently. But whatever mood had simmered between them on the bus had evaporated on the journey back—back to reality where setting up camp right inside Kitty's personal space wasn't an option without duelling bears to distract her— and the simple stew lunch that had followed had become a much stiffer affair than he would have liked. On his side as well as hers. He'd immediately started feeling self-conscious about how he'd taken advantage of her awe and wonder to get his paws all over her. Worse than the bear prints on the bus window.

Right after lunch she'd fled into her room and thrown herself into cutting her story and so he'd disappeared outside to make himself busy. Real busy.

For hours.

He shook her again. 'Kitty, time to get up.'

His eyes did what his fingers couldn't—traced across her face, her lips, that soft, dark hair that fell slightly across both. He remembered that day in Nepal when she'd run with his dogs, almost in slow motion, back and forth, her hair in her eyes. Hypnotic. He'd ached to do that, then.

'Time to get up, lazy bones.'

He spoke more loudly and gave her a firmer shove. That got her attention somewhere in dreamland. She frowned, then licked those red-flushed lips, and blinked her confusion back at him. The moments before she remembered who and where she was were like an unexpected boot to the ribs.

'Morning,' he squeezed out.

She pushed herself roughly upright with one hand and her hair away from her face with the other. 'God, is it?'

'Not literally. It's just gone four p.m.,' he added when her confusion didn't let up any. It was adorable. 'You fell asleep somewhere between lunch and now.'

Her eyes dropped to her laptop, still sitting open but sleeping as deeply as she just had been. 'Oh, no...'

'You'll get there,' he reassured, though he had no idea if that was true. 'What's your deadline?'

She blinked at him, still drowsy. 'You don't want to know...'

He was holding onto a bit of 'don't want to know' information himself... 'And if you don't get it in on time?'

'Then someone else will file my story,' she murmured, sleepily.

'And that's bad?'

'I've worked on getting that feature all year.'

'But the story still airs, right? It will just be cut by someone else.'

When exactly did a stare officially become a glare? Kitty certainly knew how to hover on the fence line.

She pulled herself up into a sitting position. 'It's my story. I wanted to edit it. The rough cut as a minimum.'

'Why? You've been paid for the trip, your expenses are covered, you've scripted it and sent them the voiceover. Does it really matter who pushes the buttons?'

'The same way it *doesn't really matter* who takes the dogs you trained and uses them to track.' She sighed, stretching and cricking her long neck. 'Editing is not a rough science. It's all about tone.'

'I didn't realise this was going to be an art piece. I thought it was a business story about a burgeoning textile industry.'

Okay, now it was officially a glare.

'It's still my story. With my name on it.' The two forks formed between her brows again. 'At least I hope so. I want it to be right.'

Her wits must have finally coalesced because she stared at the thing in his hand and finally asked the million-dollar question. 'Why are you carrying a torch?'

'Don't freak out...' As if that was going to make it any better.

She pushed to full alert. And full height. 'Tell me...'

'The power's out.'

Her skin colour lost two shades at that news. 'What? How long for?'

'No idea. It's not us. Must be at the Churchill station. Could be a couple of hours more.'

'More?' Her cry was almost a squeak. 'How long has it been out?'

'About as long as you have.' In other words, half the day.

Her panicked gaze turned to her laptop but her frantic taps on the keys didn't bring it back to life. 'It's been running on battery all this time! You have to fix this!' she cried.

'As much as I would love to gallop in all Prince Charming right now, there's really nothing I can do. Except lend you my fully charged laptop.'

Not his first preference—he would rather see her relax a little—but the panic on her face apparently brought out the chivalrous best in him.

That idea almost reassured her, except that then

her face folded again. 'No, I was three-quarters through the edit. I'd have to start over…'

Then she brightened again. 'Oh! But I was backing up on the cloud. Yay!'

He scrunched up his face, hating to burst that happy little bubble again.

'No power…' he reminded her.

'So?'

'So no Internet.'

Bubble officially burst.

'Oh, God.'

'It will probably be back on later tonight,' he said calmly, refusing to indulge her panic. 'Nothing you can do. Except get up.'

He leaned down and took both her hands and hauled her over the bed edge and onto her feet.

'What am I getting up for?' she grumbled.

'A road trip,' he volunteered. Something that wasn't at all affected by a power outage.

'Didn't we do that yesterday?' the grizzling continued.

'Not like this. Dress warm.'

He backed out of her room to the sound of her snort. 'Is there any other way to dress up here?'

'Dress *extra* warm,' he modified. 'You're going to need it.'

CHAPTER NINE

WILL WASN'T JOKING about the cold.

Kitty felt somewhere between an invalid and a princess as Will packed in layers of furs and blankets around her where she sat, awkwardly, at the front of his sled. Clearly the space was designed for something other than a human but he'd gone to the trouble of layering a few cushions down to make her more comfortable. Over in the yard his team were going berserk, barking and vocalising like mad. Once she was all tucked in, he disappeared for a moment and returned in moments, practically being towed by two of his harnessed dogs. He wrangled them over to the sled and they both turned and assumed the position. They clearly welcomed what came next.

'Bruiser and... Ernie?' she guessed, calling over their excited yips.

'The two biggest.' He nodded, wrestling the pair until he had them more or less tethered. 'You need strong dogs closest to the sled to counter its slide and take most of its weight.'

Bruiser sent a surly glare her way as he was tethered and Ernie gave her a simultaneous tail-wag and over-the-shoulder tongue-loll.

'They seem like an unlikely pair,' she commented. 'A goof and a grump.'

Will grunted. 'They're all business when the harnesses are on. Work well together.'

He was gone only moments before returning with two more dogs.

'Bose and Jango go on point,' he said as he fixed them immediately in front of the wheel pair. 'Right behind the leader. Their job is to ease the rest of the team neatly around corners.'

Kitty noted the absence of dogs between the front and back pairs. 'What "rest"?'

'Starsky and Tanner would usually run between everyone else. They and the point pair do the least physical pulling and have the least mental work to do.'

'So…more than half your team is freeloading?' She tucked her furs in more firmly and tried not to look like the biggest freeloader of them all.

He grinned. 'In a real emergency, I need the

choice of four fairly fresh search dogs when we get to our destination.'

He disappeared again and returned with Tanner trotting alongside quietly. Dexter stalked confidently on his right.

'A good lead dog is born, not trained,' he said, clipping Dexter's harness in three places to the laid-out rigging and then clipping the point pair to that. 'He has to love to be in charge naturally, to think, to stay focused. And he has to want to succeed, to keep the rest of the team moving by straining on.'

Dexter was earnest and smart. She would happily follow him into the wilderness, because he seemed like the kind of dog who would bring her out again. In fact, she had!

'Do I sense a little gender bias?'

'Nope. Females make great leads, because they aren't as easily distracted as the males.'

Right now, she was pretty darned distracted by the sight of a male bent right over connecting Dexter to his rig.

'He looks very serious about running,' she said, shifting her focus from Will's rear to Dexter's.

The dog leaned into his master's rough affection. 'It's what he lives for.'

Tanner hung close to Will's ankle but he made no move to tether the gentle dog up after he approached the sled.

'Does Tanner stay home when Starsky's busy raising pups?' she asked.

A pair wasn't a pair without two of them...

'Are you kidding? There would be a riot. Sometimes I tether him up front with Dexter. He's had a rough past so he doesn't mind the security of pairing with the alpha. Even if he'll never lead himself.'

She looked into Tanner's soft, shy eyes with a certain amount of affinity.

Neither of us the right stuff, boy...

'Shove over,' Will said, casually.

Tanner was so apoplectic about getting to ride in the sled he completely forgot to be wary of strangers and he leaped into the sled, cold damp paws and all, wiggled himself in next to her and tried hard to maintain his canine personal space. That lasted about fifteen seconds. As soon as Will hiked the dogs on, the jerk and jostle of the sled as they scrambled up to speed meant that it was easier for Tanner to slide down into a lying position than sit perched upright. He sank, and he spread, until he was pressed warmly and bodily up against Kitty.

Knowing his history, she tried not to startle him with any sudden moves but it didn't take long for her fingers to find his coat under all her blankets and she curled them into his cool fur. Underneath it wasn't cool at all.

'Well, look at you,' she cooed, scrunching her fingers. 'Travelling like a rock star.'

Tanner tipped his nose up to her and gave her what could only be described as a smile and her heart melted just a little bit.

Something about wounded animals... Of all sizes—

She turned her head just slightly until she could see Will in her peripheral vision.

And all species...

'Hike!'

The next twenty minutes was a combination of distinct hard sounds, whistles and clicks as Will urged his excited dogs onward. He perched on the sled when the team ran fast, pedalled with one foot when they slowed, and leapt off to run behind when they hit a slight rise. Every one of them had a different mushing style—some leaning left, some leaning right, legs kicking in different directions—and all of them wore little black booties to protect their feet.

Without exception, wildly lolling tongues seemed to be a vital part of their technique.

Their barks and yips finally eased into a far quieter and far steadier percussion of feet on snow, heavy pants and the icy air rushing past her ears. It was impossible to talk to Will standing behind her so Kitty just relaxed, snuggled deeper into her blankets—and her complimentary dog—and watched the forest whizz by. Once they'd been going for some minutes, they hit their rhythm and Will's involvement—and gymnastics—lessened. He stood behind her, braced wide, like some Roman chariot driver. The more the team relaxed into the run, the more Kitty did, and it became impossible not to lean back against the solid strength of Will's legs.

With his heat from behind, Tanner's to her side, all the blankets she was snuggling into, and the sinking twilight around them it wasn't long before the oxygen-saturated air did its thing to her eyelids again. In that moment, nothing else existed in the world except his strong voice, the rhythmic tattoo of twenty paws thudding on snow, the whoosh of wind against her ears and the five sets of lungs heaving in and out. No work politics. No complicated history with Will. No baggage. It was almost hypnotic; a kind of Zen-like relief that she hadn't had since she'd stood on the side of a mountain in Nepal and danced with Will's dogs.

How funny that the last true moment of peace in her life also involved dogs.

And it also involved Will…

'Woah…' he called, pulling back on the leads and drawing her eyes open. 'Woah!'

When they slowed enough, he jumped off and ran behind the sled, using his full body weight to ease the team to a halt.

Tanner sprang off and ran forward excitedly for a reunion with his friends before they'd even fully stopped.

'That was amazing!' Kitty called, her smile practically frozen to her face from the sub-zero air.

'Liked it?'

There was more than just distraction with his dog tasks in the tautness of that question. 'You thought I wouldn't?'

'Not everyone gets off on being peppered with offcast snow and showered with trailing dog saliva.' He grinned.

'Well, when you sell it like that...'

But this was Will's life. And it was almost as if he were seeking her approval.

She tumbled herself off the sled clumsily as Will set about freeing each dog from its rigging and tethering them instead to nearby trees. She carefully folded up every one of her rugs before helping Will to offload various bits of equipment from the rear of the sled.

'What's in this tub?' She groaned at the heaviest.

'They burn thousands of calories on a run,' he said. 'Need to stay hydrated and fuelled.'

The tub contained a high protein kind of mush and he mixed it with warm water from an old foam cooler. He splashed half the resulting slush into the tub's lid and put both down for the dogs to share between them. Steam rose like a thermal spring.

'Tanner's not getting any?'

'He hasn't earned it yet.'

While the five dogs gobbled their refuel, Kitty peered around at the clearing Will had brought them to. She had no way of knowing which direction they'd come but since they hadn't hit either the bay or the river then it could only be south or east. Either way it was deeper into the real Boreal, Caribou country. And wolf. And probably bear. Animals that would see their portable lights a mile off.

But as long as Will wasn't worried, she wouldn't worry.

Much.

The five dogs eventually settled but Tanner seemed to know his workday was just beginning.

'Okay,' Will said. 'Time for you to earn your keep.'

Kitty turned her focus to Tanner only to find him looking back at her with a degree of expectation. So was Will.

'Me?' she squeaked.

'I need you to play dead.'

'What?'

'Tanner's a tracking dog,' he reminded her. 'He needs some fresh meat to track.'

She stared her disbelief at him. 'You want me to go out into the forest, alone?'

'What, you never played hide-and-seek as a kid?'

On the very rare occasion that she'd had someone else to play with.

'Not amongst wild animals!'

Although that wasn't strictly true. Australia was full of creatures that could kill you, they were just smaller than the ones here. If she could crawl under the house at home, exploring amongst spiders, then she could surely find a log to hunker down behind, here.

'This is a lichen study area. Fully fenced Crown Reserve,' he added meaningfully.

She narrowed her eyes. 'I'm amazed you were able to open that gate without a support crew.'

'Ha-ha. Stop hedging.'

'No wild animals?' she checked.

'Nothing bigger than your fist.'

'And I just…hide?'

'Jog out as far as you can in three minutes. I'll take Tanner five minutes the opposite direction and then we'll find you.'

She peered out into the dark trees, her gut tight. 'And if you don't?'

'I'll find you,' he repeated, firmer, and there was something in the sure way he said it… It made her heart race.

She sagged. Hadn't he promised her something amazing? Lying cold and miserable on the forest floor scarcely counted, even if the journey out here had been pretty spectacular. 'Oh, fine. Off you go. I'll go that way.'

She chose a direction completely randomly.

'Here,' Will said, walking over to her and exchanging her scarf for his. There was a moment of biting cold and then she was wrapped in the warmth—and delicious smell—of Will Margrave. 'You'll get yours back when we find you.'

Was that supposed to be some kind of reward? Because right now, with Will's scent gently rising around her nostrils, she didn't really want her own scarf back.

Watching Will jog out of the clearing with Tanner's nose full of her scarf scent was one thing, but leaving the security and familiar comfort of the rest of the dog team armed with nothing but a torch in hand was altogether tougher. That took a few deep breaths and a couple of muttered curses. But leave she did, and she set up a gentle trot herself and wove her way between trees and crazy patches of stringy lichen and fallen logs looking for the perfect hideout.

Please don't let it be a bear den...

She found a place where one spruce had toppled against another and a whole bunch of opportunistic climber vines had twisted their way around both, creating a natural igloo of leaves and snow. She wriggled herself inside the viney cluster, out of view, checked to be sure there were no other occupants and made herself comfortable on the damp earth below.

Had she imagined that she'd be out there for hours?

It seemed as if she was barely settled before she heard Tanner's distant whiffling. And Will's encouraging calls. No words, just voice. Confident and in charge. He used a whole different set of commands and sounds for the tracking part of Tanner's training and she leaned against one tree trunk within her leafy hide, wrapped Will's scarf around her more firmly against the cold seeping up from the ground, and listened to him approach.

'Come on, boy, that's it… Friends don't let friends get lost in the forest.'

The thought that Will might consider her his friend helped warm her little hideout. So did the fact that he was talking with no idea how close he was standing to her hideout. She held her breath so that neither of them would hear it.

The snuffling grew closer. Doggie breathing

combined with a high-pitched kind of whine as Tanner tracked her closer.

'Find Kitty, buddy. Let's bring her home.'

Maybe that was something he always said when hunting for survivors, but there was something in the determined way he said it, something that wiggled in between her ribs and closed a fist around her heart.

Home.

How long had it been since she'd had one of those? She'd had houses—well, apartments, really—first in Sydney, for a while in Manchester, then in Los Angeles where CNTV posted her as their North American correspondent, but she never spent more than a few weeks at a time in any of them. Most of the time her LA apartment looked like something out of a real estate ad: clean, orderly, impersonal. Which pretty much described her life.

When you ran as hard and as far as she did when she was chasing a story, you didn't have time for homey touches. Or relationships. Or any of life's pleasures, really. You only had time for work. And accountability. And focus.

They didn't give Pulitzers out for happiness.

Will's voice grew more eager. 'Close in, buddy, close in...'

The snuffling was practically atop her and it was only a moment before a wolf-like snout intruded suddenly into her hiding place, but, instead of bursting in, Tanner withdrew again, barked, and after just a moment she heard Will's voice praising him. For signalling or marking the place, or whatever else he was trained to do. Will's praise was effusive and enthusiastic and she poked her head out in time to see them playing a raucous, twilight game of tug-of-war with a well-chewed toy. There was romping, there was rolling; whatever else it was, it was clearly the best reward Tanner could ask for.

Kitty cleared her throat. 'Is no one going to check whether I'm alive?'

The moment Will released Tanner he bound over to her and knocked her flat back into the snow, clearly expecting the adoration to continue. She was hardly about to let him down. Eventually they both ran out of steam, and Tanner lay spread half across her in the snow. She was head to toe white flakes. And only a little bit freezing.

'Good boy,' she said, rubbing that place behind

his ears she'd seen Will do with Dexter. 'Thanks for finding me.'

Will gave a signal and released him to bound off into the forest.

Kitty took the gloved hand Will extended and he pulled her onto wobbly feet. It was impossible not to fall against him in that moment before she could dig her feet more firmly into the snow but, even when she did, he was slow to release her. He pulled at one of his gloves with his teeth and then slipped his warm fingers up under her hair, resting it against the hammering pulse-point at her jaw.

It only thudded faster at the contact.

'You're alive,' he confirmed.

At least she hadn't fainted from the contact. But she was having a hard time tearing her gaze away.

'You okay?'

'Yeah. I'm good,' she breathed. 'That was fast.'

'He's a good tracker, and we didn't have a lot of distance to cover. Plus you smell really fresh.'

Her hypnotic fascination fizzled like the steam coming off the dogs' gruel. 'Thanks very much! Last time I play dead for you.'

'Fresh as in "recent".' Will laughed. 'It takes

longer to track aged scents. You were practically a hot apple pie on a window…'

He meant that as a compliment, she was sure.

'So, that's it?' she asked, turning back in the direction she thought she'd come and then realising she had no idea what direction she'd come from. 'Mission accomplished for Project Amazing?'

Will took her by the shoulders and spun her ninety degrees and then gave her a gentle nudge.

'The sledding was the first part,' he said, falling in behind her and crunching along in the snow. 'Tanner's training was the second.'

She slowed and turned to study him. What else was there to do deep in the forest a zillion miles from anywhere?

His grin hurt her heart as he sized her up.

'How are you at lighting campfires?'

When night fell in the north it really fell. Because of the angle of the sun at this time of year, twilight was slow to form but it was fast to end. People had no idea what dark really was until they'd sat in the deep Boreal halfway to the arctic circle after sunset. Even in the clearing Will had made their camp in, and even with the fire he'd managed to dig into the side of a curved fallen limb behind them, the blackness was all consuming.

But then the clouds cleared somewhat, enough to reveal a phenomenal blanket star field unravelling across the sky above them.

And suddenly she was seeing *everything* in the darkness.

'Okay, you get points for this,' she said, slightly to her side but without taking her eyes off the sky.

Will chuckled across from her, half wrapped in the same rugs and furs she'd folded so neatly earlier. The ones that weren't wrapped around her.

'I haven't seen stars like these since—'

She practically swallowed her tongue in her haste to suck her words back in.

'It's okay, Kit. You can talk about Nepal.'

'I don't mean to. But it keeps coming up. Because it's the only place we have in common.'

Although not now. Now they had Churchill, and when she'd gone from this place she would remember him working here instead of at the foot of some sad, traumatised mountain.

As she had the thought—of leaving here, leaving Will—she was suffused with an almost overwhelming grief.

'I remember the stars there so clearly,' he murmured.

'Do you miss it?'

'Parts of it. The people, the spirituality...'

'Do you think returning will ever be an option?'

He blinked up at the heavens for the longest time. Stars blinked in and out of view as dark clouds high above them powered across the sky. 'No. I don't think so.'

And so the tragedies continued...

'I'm sorry that you've lost that, too.'

He brought his eyes to hers, blinked the shadows away and refocused. 'Got anywhere special like that for you?'

She wracked her brain and was sad to find it absent of any special place. Really absent. 'I haven't really been in one place long enough...'

He turned onto his side, to face her more fully. 'What's with the crazy pace?'

'Been busy.' She shrugged.

'Have you even taken a holiday?'

'Are you kidding? With all the travelling I do the last thing I want to do is do it in my leisure time.'

'I mean just...stop. Lie on the sofa for a week, reading. Go to movie marathons. Blow it playing Candy Crush. Anything but work.'

'I get breaks between stories now and again.' Though not really. Not if she could help it. 'Like this. This is downtime.'

'If not for the fact you're thinking about work constantly, here.'

Well, not constantly. In fact, she'd started to feel guilty about how many times she hadn't thought about work since sliding down that emergency slide. Hence she'd gone really hard on the edit yesterday and last night.

'I was spontaneous in Nepal,' she reminded him. 'I stayed a whole ten days to get the rescue story.'

'Uh-huh. How often have you done it since then?'

Kitty twisted her back under her warm blankets to try and shift the pressure on her chest—as if some kind of forest spirit were sitting on her. Oxygen flowed down into her lungs, relieving the sensation, and she sank back into the blankets gratefully.

'You okay?'

'It's just…breathtaking,' she hedged, glancing up at the star field. It was too early in the night for the aurora, but she would absolutely take the phenomenal star show. Any day.

'So, tell me about work,' Will muttered.

She didn't shift her eyes from the stars. 'What about it?'

'Why you push yourself so hard. What you're doing it for.'

Her ribs shrank into each other. 'Surely, a man like you understands wanting to be the best at what you do.'

'A man like me?'

'Driven, ambitious, determined.'

'Is that how you see me?'

She rushed to undo the offence she could hear in his reply. 'Those are all good things in my book.'

'I guess I am determined. And possibly driven. Never really thought of myself as ambitious though.'

'You say that like it's a disease,' she muttered. 'I see it as a virtue.'

'I guess you would…'

She took a long breath and reminded herself that she'd been wanting to have this kind of conversation with Will Margrave for years. She didn't necessarily get to pick the topic. Or the timing.

'Success makes me happy.'

'Happiness makes you happy,' he corrected.

'Success just makes you too busy to notice that you're not. Trust me.'

'Really, Will? You're going to lecture me about working to the exclusion of everything else? Isn't that exactly what you're doing here in Churchill? Keeping busy enough that you don't notice the loneliness?'

'My work saves lives,' he defended, darkly.

'And mine's trivial by comparison?'

'I didn't say that.' Will puffed into the air.

But he had no problem leading her to admitting it; that compared to the kinds of stories she used to tell, the ones she told now really were pretty inconsequential. But most of the time she did a fine old job of deluding herself.

Occupational necessity.

'We don't all have the vocational calling that you've had, Will.' Trained since he was a boy by the search-and-rescue uncle who raised him. Really, what chance he was going to be anything but a rescuer, too? 'For me, work actually earns the name.'

Blue eyes blazed into hers, really seeking. 'It didn't used to.'

Shame stole any reply—at her thoughtless words and because he was essentially right.

He studied the skies for a while. 'I'm sorry if I hit a sore point.'

'It's not.' *Pfff.* 'I just don't appreciate having to defend myself.'

He easily brushed her defensiveness off. 'Please. You love defending yourself. Those long, late-night discussions we had about just about anything. I sometimes wondered if you took the conflicting view simply to get me worked up.'

Just how transparent had she been five years ago? Will had the sexiest brain she'd ever met; back then, she'd debated with him ardently in lieu of getting to touch him—it was all she'd had.

The fire popped loud enough to startle Ernie, and Will freed himself of blankets and went to tend it.

'If you could go back in time six years, would you still go to Nepal?' she asked.

He poked at the fire for the longest time. 'Yeah. But I wouldn't have taken Marcella.'

'To save her from the quake?'

His poking paused. 'To save her from discovering who she was. And who she wasn't.'

'What do you mean?'

'Marcella had this firm view of who she was, who she wanted to be—the bohemian artist, the loving wife living in this great, spiritual place. She married me, we moved to the Himalayas, had this great traditional Nepalese house on a lake… It should have been perfect. But, the reality was she was more like her parents and sisters than she knew and, in some ways, discovering that killed her long before the quake did.'

Who she was… Who she wanted to be… Kitty curled deeper into her blankets—wasn't that exactly what she'd spent five years doing? Trying to be someone different. Someone manufactured? The kind of someone who had a terrifically successful and glamorous career. Enviable, even?

What if she was no more suited to the lifestyle she'd created than Marcella had turned out to be to hers?

He turned to face her. 'What about you, Kitty? Would *you* still go to Nepal, if you had a do-over?'

'Yes.' Bam. Just like that. Though she'd never given the idea a moment's thought.

His gaze grew thoughtful. 'Even with how it ended up?'

'Yes.' She didn't need to consider. No matter how she felt about leaving it. 'Nepal was…freedom, for me. No obligations, no expectations, total creative freedom. You and Marcella, the people in your village, just accepted me for exactly who I was. Even your dogs welcomed me.'

He grunted. 'Don't read too much into it, Kitty. Dogs are pretty accepting.'

Don't read too much into it... Was that a warning to her now?

She frowned. 'Were you always this much of a killjoy?'

His teeth glowed in the firelight. 'I respect you too much to lie to you.'

A fist gave her heart a quick squeeze. Or was it her lungs? 'Really? I never would have guessed.'

That surprised him. 'My questions are designed to know you better, not to find fault.'

The same breathlessness that she'd endured in Nepal hit her now, even in this oxygen-rich forest. 'Why would you want to know me better?'

He hung his head as he agitated the fire then turned it sideways to peer back at her across the clearing. 'Because I feel like I missed out on something, back in Nepal.'

Thump, thump, thump.

That was exactly what she felt. But hearing him say it left her almost faint. 'Careful what you wish for, Will. You might find you don't like what you find, at all.'

Hadn't he already said she'd changed?

He pushed to his feet, into shadow, so that she couldn't quite find his gaze, but his earnest gaze stole every bit of breath she'd managed to suck in as he stepped forward into the fire's circle of light.

'I doubt that,' he murmured.

She wanted to answer—some terrifically witty response—but, nope, there wasn't enough air left in her cells let alone her lungs. All she could do was stare into the sparkling depths of his eyes and wonder what it would be like to swim strokes in the icy blue there.

As she watched they flicked down to her parted lips and back again. 'You're an enigma to me, Kitty Callaghan. And I've always enjoyed puzzles.'

She wanted to warn him that she was more puzzle than he knew. She was one of those boxes with hidden mechanisms and cryptic clues and booby traps if you pressed the wrong place. She wanted to but she didn't, because the moment he stared at her lips all she could think about was what it would be like to kiss him. To taste him and breathe him in.

After all this time.

And in that moment she knew that she'd been

wanting that since the very first moment she'd met him. More than just about anything else in her life.

'Did you see those science teachers this morning?' she asked, desperate for something neutral to break the energy stretching from him to her. 'How passionate they were about their work?'

'I didn't need to see them. I could breathe it.'

'Is that how you feel about running your dogs? Does it give you that kind of buzz? Or is it just… routine, now?'

'When we discover someone,' he started, 'it's the most natural of highs. Adrenaline. Excitement. Elation. Pride. Grief if they haven't made it. Sorrow that we weren't quicker.'

His voice carried a hundred memories. Good and bad.

'But recovery moments are few and far between in search and rescue. Ninety per cent of my job is mundane stuff like training, preparation, equipment checks. But even the mundane bits still interest me, or I wouldn't do it. Life is too short.'

It had been a long while since the mundane parts of her job had interested her. Even some of the cool parts—the international travel, the public profile—no longer excited her.

'Do you remember why you started doing it?' she pushed, without really understanding why. She just needed to know if she was the only one feeling this way.

'Yes. Because of my parents.'

The ones who'd gone out sailing off Newfoundland and never come back. Marcella had told her. No wonder he handled death so bravely with that kind of formative training.

'And do you still feel the same about it?'

Will's face creased with curiosity. 'Yes.'

There we go... She fell to silence. What else was there to say?

'Are you having doubts?' Will nudged. 'About your job?'

'No.' Producing stories was all she knew. She'd been doing it since she graduated. Who was she if she wasn't Super-Correspondent? Right down to the cape and lettered chest. 'Maybe.'

'Is there anything else you want to do?'

She tipped her face to the sky where the clouds were closing back in, backlit by the rising moon. 'I couldn't start over, after everything I've given up...'

Although the opportunity was getting further

away with every year she sank into her career. Just like Mei.

'What things?'

'Friendships. Those close relationships that need nurturing to keep them alive.' She shuffled in her blankets.

'What about romantic relationships?' he asked softly.

She turned to him. Forty-eight hours ago she never would have had this conversation with Will, risked it. But forty-eight hours ago they were still virtual strangers.

'At first I avoided getting to know anyone beyond one date just in case I found myself—' repeating the mistakes of the past '—getting too involved. And then there was no point even going on that first date because it only led to disappointment.'

Not to mention the lurking shadow of a man none of them could hope to match.

'A home,' she went on. 'Who knew I'd start hankering for that? I return to an entryway full of mail, no car because it would sit on the street more than drive on it. I don't even have potted plants in my apartment because I'm not there often enough to keep them alive.'

And if she couldn't care for a potted plant what hope for the children she'd probably never have? Marriages took time. Children took time. And energy. And total focus. How could she ever achieve that with her punishing schedule?

'So walk away. It's just a job, Kitty. You'll find something else.'

'I can't walk away. I'm not done.'

'When will you be?'

She stared at him.

'Senior correspondent? Producer of the show? Network head? President? When will you wake up and think "I'm done. I've made it."? And what will you have missed on the way?'

It was only the deep compassion she saw in his face that kept her from getting up and walking off. That and the fact she had no idea where they even were.

'People don't walk away from fruitful careers.' She sighed, curling her fingers firmly in her fists. Certainly not without something better to go to.

'People do. All the time. This town is full of them. Tell me—' he leaned in '—what would you do with your life if *you* could go back six years? If you never started working for CNTV. If you weren't answerable to anyone but yourself.'

How could she answer that? Who was she, even, six years ago? It was almost impossible to remember. She wasn't about to tell Will her most secret fantasies of pottering in a home studio making films *she* cared about, mothering a clutch of kids by a man who looked dangerously like him—someone exceptional, someone bright and capable and not afraid to sit up all night talking when the passion took them. Someone with their own priorities who wasn't afraid to give her a high place amongst them.

'It's a moot point, Will. No one gets to press "reset" in the real world.'

'I did,' he reminded her. 'I got rather a big shove, if you recall. I don't want to see the universe shaking you quite that hard to get yours, Kitty.'

She dropped her gaze. 'I appreciate your concern. But I'm fine.'

Her career—such as it was—had served her well all this time. It was hardly perfect but it put food on the table and gave her a focus. What exactly did he imagine she would do with all that time if not work?

Hopes of anything more were just that—dangerous hopes.

Will's eyes had become dark shadows in the

fire's dim glow and she realised it was little more than coals now despite his prodding. How late it was getting and how cold she was.

And not all of it was from outside.

She'd woken up in a lot of new places in her time but at least she knew what she had, and she knew what she was doing no matter where she was. She might not have been setting the world on fire as she'd once dreamed, but a monthly pay-cheque had a lot to recommend it.

She tucked her blankets more firmly around her and assured him.

'Truly. I'm fine.'

CHAPTER TEN

IT WAS A LONG, silent journey back to the cabin under the thick cover of cloud. Will put his trust in the dogs' night vision and they ran steadily along, though not as fast as they'd made the outbound journey. His heart just wasn't in it. He glanced down at Kitty, and the headlamp fixed to his forehead did the whole searchlight thing where she and Tanner squirrelled under the rugs, her hand gently stroking the dog's nose where he'd laid it across her lap.

That was a first. For both of them.

Ahead, Dexter wavered and began to show interest in things off to the side. The rest of the team followed him and the sled moved dangerously towards the snow-buried foliage lining the track. Will shook himself out of the hypnotic stupor caused by the dogs' steady *one-two, one-two* pace and focused on communicating with his lead.

'Haw, Dexter!' he called into the night, half as loud as he usually would.

The rig straightened up and all five dogs hit their regular rhythm again.

It had been two years since his mind had been this addled. The last time had been the shock of the landslide—it had just robbed him of the ability to do any mental processing for weeks. Fortunately, there had been no shortage of work to keep him busy. He'd driven his remaining dogs near into the ground with the endless recovery work and it had only been when the demolition had started that he'd eased back. He hadn't been able to fully check out but he'd at least been able to function.

He was every bit as vacant right now, but for very different reasons. That time it was losing his whole world.

This time it was finding it—finding Kitty. Something he'd not ever let himself want. Yet here she was, in his sled. In his cabin. In his life, albeit temporarily. And there was no good reason that she couldn't be there this time.

Except for his fear.

There weren't many moments quite as compelling as catching yourself responding to the impassioned glitter in the eyes of the woman sitting across the table from your wife. Awkward! As soon as he'd caught himself, he'd vowed he would never let it happen again.

Yet here it was…happening again. Just because Marcella was gone now didn't make indulging his simmering hormones any less risky a proposition. Kitty had an international career to be getting on with—she could hardly pull up stakes and replant them here, a thousand miles from the nearest big city. Not without regretting it later. The last thing he needed in this world was another woman looking to escape her own life.

Look how the last time had turned out.

The glowing cabin approached and Will leapt off the back of the sled to haul it to a stop. 'Woah…'

Kitty disentangled herself from all the rugs. 'Looks like the power is back on.'

Which meant she'd be working all evening. Which meant she'd hide out in her room again.

Which was probably a good thing.

He grunted. 'Looks like.'

It took him twenty minutes after she'd gone in to de-harness the dogs and give them another small feed to replenish their energy before he let them out for a fast forage break, then into the safety of the cabin for the night. They immediately separated to lie in their favourite corners of the house.

Somehow the little cabin just absorbed them all, like shadows. He stripped out of all his layers, boosted up the fire and got it roaring again and then restarted all the appliances that needed re-setting after a power outage.

Immediately his landline started blinking.

He headed to his kitchen and pressed the message recall button on the way past.

'This is a message for Ms Kitty Callaghan,' the voice said before identifying itself as being from Kitty's airline. Will froze in the middle of pouring himself a glass of water. 'Ma'am, we're happy to advise that you have been re-seated on a Winnipeg-bound flight departing Churchill at noon tomorrow. If you can please check in one hour before, that will give us time to screen your luggage and get you validated. Thank you very much, see you tomorrow no later than eleven.'

Beep.

A chill worse than the one he endured standing on the back of the sled in winter soaked right through him and he let the water jug sag to the benchtop.

Kitty was leaving—he glanced at his watch—fourteen hours from now.

Fourteen hours and he would be waving her off

as he had five years ago, with a polite smile and a carefully blank expression. Just as he was getting to know her again. No, not 'again', just as he was getting to know her for the first time, properly.

He pressed down with both sets of palms on his benchtop.

Then again it was also fourteen hours and he could go back to his regular life; his predictable, ordered existence with his dogs. Back to being accountable to no one but himself. Back to a warm, silent cabin in a deep, peaceful woods where no one conjured the past every five minutes. Where no one challenged him to be different. Or better. So maybe it was for the best.

Quit while they were ahead.

'Kitty?' he called, abandoning his water in favour of letting her know she needed to start packing. 'Kit?'

The silence drew him up the hallway towards her room. As he passed the bathroom, the door sprung open and she stepped out and ran square into him, all clean and damp from her shower. All warm and pink and cosy in her cute pyjamas.

His gut tightened at the soapy freshness.

'Oh! Sorry,' she laughed before remembering that she was annoyed at him for his insensitive probing, and he tried to imagine ever getting bored of that sound. Her voice cooled a little. 'Did you want something?'

'Your airline called.' He coughed his throat clear. 'You're scheduled for noon tomorrow.'

That look on her face... Those moments before she managed to mask it—that was exactly what he imagined his expression had been on hearing the airline's message.

Shock. Denial. Resignation. Acceptance.

Like the stages of grief played out over seconds.

'Oh. Great.' But she didn't move, and those lines between her brows didn't lessen any. Whatever she'd used on her hair, or her skin, it wafted up to tease his senses. 'Um, okay...I guess I should pack then.'

Did she mean to make it that much of a question? Her grey eyes lifted and found his. Almost as if she was giving him an opportunity to disagree.

'Guess so,' he said carefully, taking another step back.

She gathered her bathroom things more closely to her chest and turned for her room. Before she disappeared into it, he spoke up.

'Hey, Kitty...?'

She turned much quicker than his gentle query required, her eyes lit by something he couldn't define. 'Yes?'

Was she still waiting for him to disagree?

'Give me your towel. I'll lay it out by the fire. So you don't pack it damp.'

'Oh.' The indefinable something extinguished. 'Thank you.'

Had gratitude ever sounded so insincere? What exactly had she been hoping he was going to say?

Her hand brushed his as she passed the towel to him and the softness of her fingertips against his own struck him. They were so different. She moved in high places, travelled the world and had interview appointments with CEOs of the biggest corporations. She had the hands of a musician or a writer...or a news correspondent.

He had calluses as rough as the pads on his dogs' feet and his only appointments for the foreseeable future were a twice-daily obligation at a remote flagpole.

No matter what kind of professional rut she was in, staying in Churchill was no more realistic an option than Marcella living in Nepal had turned out to be. Great in principle, exciting and novel in planning, but hard work and isolated in practice. And it wouldn't be long before she was regretting giving up that fine career. Or resenting him for being part of it.

Just like Kitty's philosophy on dating… So much easier to just not even start.

Not that this was easy.

He dragged a chair nearer to the fire and draped her damp towel across its back, and that same smell that had teased his nostrils in the hallway set up a full assault now. It filled the room with some flowery scent and managed to subjugate the usual smell of spruce wood, leather and dog.

Who knew how much time he lost immersing himself in that smell? But somewhere in there he sank into his own leather rocker.

'Will?' Kitty asked quietly from the doorway.

He shot from his chair, as his uncle had raised him, and turned to face her. She'd thrown a thin sweater on over the pyjamas, which went some way to reducing the cling against her skin, but the soft fabric did nothing to lessen the cosy, relaxed feel he got just looking at her and the pale blue did amazing things to her eyes.

'I was wondering if you were planning on eating?' she said. 'I know it's late…'

Shame kneed him in the guts. It was ten p.m.

and he'd only taken food for the dogs with them on their evening sled ride. She must be starving.

He really had been living with wolves too long.

'I could eat,' he said casually, forcing the shame down. Though he really wasn't that interested. The last supper of a condemned man and all that. 'What do you feel like?'

They did the whole, awkward whatever-you-like/no-whatever-*you*-like dance and, in the end, he pulled together some whipped eggs and Parmesan before gently sizzling it into a fluffy omelette. At the final stage, he drizzled butter over the lot before searing it on both sides and sliding half each onto two plates. It was all very French.

'Marcella teach you that?' Kitty asked from right behind him, making him fumble the pan at a crucial moment.

But he recovered. 'Her grandmother, actually. It was a family favourite.'

She perched on a stool at the end of his kitchen bench, her long legs crossed casually, forking mouthfuls of the impromptu dinner in at a pretty steady rate. Either she really was starving or she was trying to avoid conversation. Finally, she carefully laid her fork onto her empty plate and looked up.

'I'll be sorry to leave, tomorrow, Will.'

Nope. No, you won't. You need to get back to your world before one of us does something stupid...

'I hope I've met my obligations regarding northern hospitality,' he said.

Her smile didn't reach her eyes. 'Thoroughly. Rogue polar bears, Halloween, dog-sledding. What more could a girl from Down Under ask for?'

The gentle tease was almost as good as the waft of soapy scent. It tingled wherever her words fell. The way snowflakes felt on bare skin.

In fact, his senses were almost fully engaged by Kitty: her distinctive scent, the sight of her all soft and just showered, the tinkle of her teasing laugh, the brush of her soft skin against his. Pretty much all he was missing now was taste.

And that little question mark would never be answered.

No matter how it plagued him.

'I'm glad I got to see you,' she said quietly, eyes serious. 'To set things right between us.'

That smacked just a little bit too much of closure, which, in turn, smacked just a little bit too much of goodbye. Knowing something had to

happen and wanting it to happen weren't necessarily the same thing. Sometimes you did the hard
thing for the right reason—even though it felt all
kinds of wrong.

How long had it taken him to learn that? Maybe
if he'd manned up and sent Marcella home she
would still be breathing and laughing and painting today.

'To undo what I did?' he tested, wanting to keep
her out here with him as long as possible.

Her eyebrows dropped, then her lashes followed
suit.

'I didn't like leaving Nepal,' she said. 'And I
didn't like not knowing what was happening with
you. That you were okay. Stay in touch, going forward, huh?'

She sounded very resigned, which only served
to make him more depressed.

But he fought it. This was what he wanted. 'You
know where I am. Email will always be open.'

But she wouldn't use it. The moment her wheels
left the runway she'd start retreating back into the
real world. And, in the real world, Kitty Callaghan
and Will Margrave didn't stay in touch. He knew
them both well enough to be sure of that.

It was just too fraught.

Awareness zinged back and forth between them, almost tangible enough to feel. They'd never been short of chemistry and it was making itself known now. It only served to validate the distance he'd kept five years ago. And was forcing now.

Look what happened when he let his guard down.

'Well…' he hinted, glancing up the hall. Putting himself out of his misery.

Something behind her gaze flattened and it killed him to be responsible for that. Once again.

The hard thing for the right reason…

Kitty needed to be heading south again. Back to her world. Back to the life she'd been steadily working on. That life didn't include a remote little bear town and it didn't include a search-and-rescue hermit or his dogs.

'Yes. I should get packing.'

Packing meant leaving. Which he wanted, but you wouldn't know that by the thud of his heart.

'No editing tonight?'

She looked startled enough that he wondered if she'd even remembered her story waiting to be cut. 'Looks like I'll be back in the hotel tomorrow afternoon. I should be able to get it finished then.'

Without him and his endless outdoor distractions. 'In time for your deadline?'

Something flickered across the back of her gaze. 'Close enough.'

She didn't exactly look enthused by that, but she slipped down off the stool and hovered in the opening to the kitchen.

'Thanks for the eggs.' That simple sentence seemed to hold so much more meaning.

'You're welcome,' he said, trying hard to invest just as much in his. 'See you in the morning.'

She hesitated, lips parted, but then her hips turned, her shoulders followed and finally her face turned for her bedroom.

Her eyes were the last thing to leave him.

Kitty sagged against her closed bedroom door, forcing her breath in and out. Mastering it. It had threatened to overwhelm her out in the kitchen where every minute that passed was a minute closer to her departure in the morning. Thank goodness for the training that had taught her how to regulate her breathing so that she could present to camera, live, even after dashing across a war zone. That was all that had kept her conversation flowing while her mind had been so busy crying out for Will.

If her career had taught her anything, it was how to fake it until she could make it.

She wasn't ready to leave. She wasn't even sure she *could* be ready. Four days ago fate had bounced her down an emergency slide in Churchill and she'd thought it was simply safe harbour. She'd had no inkling that she would find a thing here in this isolated, insular place that she'd thought she'd never have. Ever.

A second chance. With Will.

And she'd just left that second chance standing, all handsome and rugged, in the kitchen. Waving her off with a relieved smile. Much like the one he'd worn in Nepal.

Panic welled up around her ankles. Had she done it again? Outstayed her welcome... Misread the signals... Had she assumed that Will was as happy to have her stay as she had started to feel here? He'd joked about northern hospitality but was that what all this had been?

Obligation?

He certainly wasn't making any grand efforts to stay in touch.

You know where I am. Email will always be open...

Yeah, not exactly compelling evidence.

She paced her tiny room, shaking out the anxiety through flapping hands. As much as she didn't want to pack, she needed to be moving, otherwise she was going to sprint back down that hallway and say something that she really shouldn't. She and Will had only just become friends. After five years. She wasn't about to blow that by blurting out her feelings just because she lacked self-discipline. She'd survived the humiliation once before—just—but only by throwing her life totally off orbit and into a new direction. If he rejected her again she really wasn't sure what was left to do to help her get past it.

What she *was* going to do was pack, head back to some comfortable, anonymous hotel in Manitoba's capital, cut her story and file it with CNTV, get on a connecting flight for Los Angeles, and get on with the rest of her life. A new story. A new country. A new focus.

The sort of life that was just so noisy it drowned out the weeping of her lovesick heart.

She froze, a stone settling deep in her gut as she sank down onto her mattress.

Love?

Please, no, not again.

Hadn't she learned a thing from past experience? She couldn't love Will Margrave any more now than she had in Nepal. There might no longer be a marriage standing between them but nothing else had changed about their relationship. She honestly didn't think she could survive another dose of his pity.

Kitty started tossing things into her suitcase carelessly, abandoning her finely developed packing system—everything rolled, everything in its place—and scouring the room for anything she'd left behind. Normally she would take her equipment on as hand luggage but, nope, she threw that in as well, forcing her belongings—like her feelings—behind the very sturdy, very final suitcase zipper.

Ziiiiip.

That sound was a symbol for her life. It meant a new start. A new adventure. It meant flights and planning and research and interviews, and all the things she did that kept her so busy three hundred and sixty-five days a year. That zipper had become a marker for the passing years of her life. One after the next after the next…

She sagged back onto the end of her bed.

So many years. And what did she have to show for it? No home. Precious few friends. Zero romantic relationships.

But one hell of a résumé.

Only one of those things was going to take her to the top.

She stared at her trembling hands with a curious detachment. As if they weren't even hers. Then, finger by finger, she curled them, then flexed them, then wrapped them around the nearest loose item and tossed it into her suitcase.

These cases weren't going to pack themselves.

CHAPTER ELEVEN

'WAKE UP, SLEEPYHEAD.'

Kitty twitched and roused and let herself be dragged—reluctantly—out of slumber to the sound of Will's voice. There were certainly worse ways to start a day. But that cosy pleasure only lasted moments before the cold reality intruded.

Today was the day she would leave Churchill. And leave Will.

'Kitty?'

She rolled onto her side and opened her eyes. Didn't they just do this? 'Why is it so dark?'

'It's night time,' he whispered. 'Well, morning, really. Very early.'

'Why am I awake?' she grumbled.

Mornings really weren't her forte. Especially not when she'd lain awake so long angsting about her future.

'I have a surprise for you,' Will said, a little louder. Every word brought her closer to consciousness.

'In the middle of the night?'

'Look out your window.'

If there wasn't a wolf standing there...with a bear...riding a moose...she was going to be mightily cranky. She'd never in her life slept as much or as well as here in Will's cabin and a rude midnight awakening was not high on her list of must-dos before leaving today.

She peered through her lashes at the Boreal beyond the picture window. It was its usual mass of darkness. But there was something else, a kind of glow hovering over all of it.

She pushed herself higher and craned her neck. 'Is there a fire?'

But no, that made no sense. Fires were orange. She squinted to get a better look.

The glow started on the horizon, like the urban glow of a city—a far bigger city than Churchill would ever be—and far greener.

'I thought the port was in the other direction?'

It spread like a gas, unevenly and fast changing, wiping out all but the brightest stars and back-lighting the clumps of cloud still lingering in the sky until they, too, glowed a sick kind of emerald.

She shot up into a seated position, eyes still firmly on the sky. 'Wait... Is that the aurora?'

'The corona has been maxing all week,' Will murmured. 'But it's been happening behind the veil of thick cloud we've had since you arrived. I let the dogs out for a nature break just now and saw that they'd lifted.'

Maxing and coronas and veils made no sense but the colours swilling across the sky made perfect, painful sense. Because making the decision to go hadn't been hard enough. The treacherous fates had thrown in a curve ball at the eleventh hour.

She shot to the window and pressed her hands onto the freezing glass. It startled her into full awareness.

'I was hoping it would still be pulsing,' he said from the darkness behind her. 'That you'd get to see it. I thought you wouldn't mind being woken...'

By the moment, the green gas thickened and gathered until it formed twisted ropes of colour that warped and wove across the sky.

'Will...' The warm whisper of his name on the glass formed a pool of mist. Then she spun. 'Can we go outside?'

'It's freezing,' he warned. 'Properly freezing. That's why visibility is so good tonight.'

'I'll put on everything I haven't packed,' she vowed.

She grabbed her sweater from dinner, the jeans she'd laid out for the morning, her insulated parka, her beanie and her warmest socks and gloves and pulled the lot on over her thick pyjamas. Then she turned back out to the Boreal to reconsider just how cold it might be before hauling her thick eiderdown off Will's spare bed and throwing that around her shoulders as well.

'Come on, Michelin Man,' he joked.

She practically waddled down the hallway behind him.

She'd sat on the outdoor sofa on Will's timber deck just once in five days, and only long enough to re-lace her boots. It would have been startlingly cold to sit on it if not for the fact that she didn't, walking instead to the middle of the deck and peering upwards.

'Oh, good Lord...'

The colour and intensity of auroras diminished with every degree of latitude you got away from it. Further south, human eyes saw the lights totally differently from how the cameras, there, captured it. She'd only ever seen *these* lights—proper

Northern Lights—in magazine shoots. Yet here they were in all their multicoloured glory.

Even for puny primate eyes.

'Take a seat, Kitty,' Will rumbled. 'You've got plenty of time. The sky scanner shows the clouds are still lifting.'

She sank down onto the sofa and tucked herself in more firmly against the cold from below.

Overhead, the strands of colour danced and flowed between Earth and the endless spreading star field. The few remaining clouds looked like sea ice floating on the surface of a dark ocean of night. And the aurora were schools of luminous plankton swarming below the ice. The longer Kitty stared, the harder it became to distinguish sky from ocean; as if she were looking down on it, rather than up.

'It's so beautiful…'

And so bright it was making her eyes water, because surely she was too old and too seasoned to get choked up by the sight of the Northern Lights.

'I'm glad the sky cleared enough while you're still here,' he said, hopping from foot to foot.

She might have put on half her wardrobe but Will was only wearing what he'd come and woken her in and his parka hastily thrown over the top.

'Here,' she ordered. 'Come and get under the quilt.'

He hesitated and she wondered for a pained heartbeat whether he would rather freeze to death than sit that close to her and maybe have her get the wrong impression, but then he moved and joined her. She lowered the blanket and laid it across their legs.

His agitation slowly eased just as Bose's had on the tower all those days ago.

And then, as the aurora swirled and churned, threads of the prettiest pink began to form, merging with the green in a way that just looked so… right…in the sky. Yet at the same time so incredibly alien. A tortured, twisted night rainbow. Against the stark shape of the Tamarack and spruce trees, it was like a fairy-tale world reflected perfectly in the mounds of white snow piled up everywhere.

'Now you're shivering,' Will muttered, throwing the quilt off himself.

'I'm sure we can get both of us under…'

He glanced at her, then seemed to decide something. 'Stand up. Come on… Up.'

She stumbled to her feet as Will did. He took the thick quilt off her and wrapped it around himself like a giant towel before sinking back into the sofa corner and stretching one long leg down its length. The other fell to the deck. Kitty glanced at the bare sofa between his denim thighs.

'Once in a lifetime, Kit,' he said, a green glow ebbing and flowing on his face. 'I'm sure you'll survive.'

He was talking about the lights, she knew, but the other life experience he was offering her...

She wasn't about to pass that up.

Besides, without the quilt she was as cold as he must have been just now.

She took a deep breath and sat in the vacant space in front of Will. Immediately he folded the fluffy thing around both of them, his arms crossing across her chest the way they had in the bus out on the tundra. With his body heat behind and the thick downy quilt in front she was in a warm little cocoon of heaven.

'God, that's better,' he groaned.

Uh, yeah, it really was. For reasons that had nothing to do with the temperature. As warmth soaked into her, it was hard to fight the sensation that this was how she should have been living life all along—with someone's arms around her.

Will's arms.

His heart beat steadily against her shoulder and she was glad their positions weren't reversed so that he couldn't feel the puppy-like peppering of her own excited one. He might not buy that it was just the lights getting her pulse up.

The aurora began to dance in earnest as if to their combined rhythm.

It didn't take long for her neck to start aching from the constant head-tilt and so she settled back against Will's chest and rested the back of her head on his shoulder. He adjusted his position slightly to make space for her there. It occurred to her, vaguely, to be embarrassed by the picture they presented but she would deal with humiliation later. Right now she was just going to enjoy the light show while she had the chance. And the touching. She fitted perfectly into the curves and dips of his torso. And his padded shoulder was like a comfy, masculine pillow.

A forest gust sprang up and battered against their warm little igloo, blowing a few of her curls loose across her face.

'I got it,' Will murmured against her ear.

He liberated one strong hand from the quilt and brushed the curls away with the bared knuckle of his little finger, tucking them more securely under the thick fold of her beanie. When he was done, she wiggled back up against him, until his jaw rested against the wool he'd just patted flat.

If the gods sent out a bolt of lightning through all that swilling green and struck her down right now, she'd be pretty darned happy to go.

Like this; surrounded, protected.

Loved.

Or at least a plausible facsimile of it. It wasn't real, she knew that, but she could enjoy that fantasy for just a few moments, couldn't she?

The sky warped and wove as she watched, though even that failed to upstage the sensations beginning to form under the quilt insulating them like a layer of snow. Behind her, Will's chest rose and fell more quickly and he brushed his jaw absently along her beanie, first in subtle strokes timed with the swirls of green and then more purposeful, more bold. As if testing to see what she'd do.

About all she *could* do was lean into every stroke and sigh softly as the electrical energy high above them suddenly seemed to swill all around them, in and between their limbs. Will's fingers tightened their hold on the quilt, pressing his arms more firmly around her and bringing her closer to the hot breath she'd been quietly enjoying against her ear.

And then he stopped—froze, really—poised on a gaping precipice. As if he was too afraid to take the next step. Or as if he was fighting some great internal battle.

Every cell in her body refocused on what was happening on this sofa rather than in the heavens above.

'Will…'

Even that single syllable couldn't do much more than form as a tiny sigh in her throat.

But a sigh was all he needed…

One moment, the place below her beanie—the place he'd tucked her curls—was icy cold from exposure to the frosty air and the next it was alive with wet heat as his lips pressed there, firm and determined. Just once, but roaming. Her chest heaved at the contact and she leaned into his kiss, her eyes fluttering shut.

'Kitty…'

She must have met him halfway because as she breathed in he was there, mouthing her throat experimentally and, by the time she breathed out, his lips sought their way across her jaw and she was twisting her neck to make it happen. The gentle rasp of his scrappy beard growing back in tantalised the cold-nipped skin of her face right before his lips made proper contact.

Kissing Will was like a homecoming. The correction of a years-old error. It felt *meant* that it was witnessed by these cosmic bands of mystery.

Kissing Will was right.

It joined them in a way she'd never let herself imagine, but had always, always wanted. It warmed her from within. And it said one thing...

Home.

She breathed him in, filled her lungs with him; with the microscopic traces that made Will who he was. They sent her own chemicals into a frenzy. He pressed in closer, shoring up the kiss, and twisted further to bring her into the warmth and safety of his body. One hand abandoned its quilt duties to curl beneath her head, holding her steady for his lips, and the other one forked in under her beanie to tangle in the curls there. As if he'd been wanting to do that for ever. Their covers fell partly away but their friction generated such an inferno it didn't matter.

She was never leaving these arms.

Not now that she'd finally found her way into them.

But a girl had to breathe…

She sighed against his lips. Against his smile. She'd been functioning on extra oxygen for so many days now, it bought her precious extra moments without before she had to tear her mouth from Will's.

'I knew it would be like this.'

'Knew it? Or hoped it?' He nuzzled against her ear, not entirely steady.

Feared it.

She trembled as the frigid air met the wet trail from his lips, and his arms tightened. 'You weren't mine to want back in Nepal.'

Some secret part of her worried that he still wasn't. That this was just a moment conjured by the other-worldly lights still swirling overhead and by his long years of isolation. That it would end when the lights did.

He pulled back on a lazy grin. 'You can want me tonight. Knock yourself out.'

Something about his words rattled in her brain— zinged, really, as if they were trying to get her attention—but her head was way too foggy for actual conversation.

In lieu of speech, he leaned into her again—over her—and reclaimed her mouth with his. Slow and teasing. Smiling and deadly. Hot when everything around them was so very cold. It drove all sense clear out of her tiny mind.

They kissed—and they kissed—until the enormous moon was three-quarters of the way across the night sky.

'I could do this for hours.' He sighed, pulling back and sagging next to her. Close enough for her to see two tiny mirrors of the Northern Lights reflected in his smoky gaze.

'I think we already have.' She chuckled.

'I meant the hours we have left,' he said, still clouded by their heady kissing.

She lifted her face and stared at him.

'Before your flight,' he clarified, as though all the kissing had sucked the sense out of her.

In those few words, everything that had happened in Nepal came crashing back into focus—all the feelings she'd tried to suppress, struggled to ignore, when Will had sent her away the first time—and she realised what a monumental mistake she had made.

He was letting her go? Again?

She struggled against his warm body to sit up, which left Will with no option but to release her. He pushed up to sitting, too. 'Kitty—?'

'I just need…a moment.' To sort this out in her head. Why it should matter. Why it *did* matter.

She'd just talked herself into reaffirming her commitment to her career. So, getting on the plane and heading south shouldn't have been such a terrible concept. But some part of her—a part that had been frozen, asleep for a really long time—secretly wanted it to matter very much to Will. For him to rail and protest and mourn the coming dawn. For him to want her *not* to go.

Rather than accepting it quite so…readily.

She scrambled to set her feet back on the frost-crunched deck.

'Kitty—'

'What are we doing?' she cried, wrapping her arms around her torso. Her heart hammered against her arm, even faster now than when she'd been coiled in Will's embrace.

'What we've wanted to do for five years?'

She spun on him. 'But why? Just hours before I fly away from you. What was this for you, just a nice way to pass the time?'

She should ask herself the same question.

'You leave in the morning,' he urged. 'What other chance will we have? And then there you were all warm and sleepy literally in my arms under this gorgeous sky...'

'So you thought you'd just lob a grenade into the beautiful moment by kissing me?'

He took a wounded step back from her rising anger. 'I thought I was making it more beautiful.'

She struggled against the need to sag. Because— God help her—he *had* made it more beautiful.

'Kitty, what's wrong?'

Screw it. Acquiescing graciously might have saved her dignity five years ago but it hadn't done anything to help her heart. She wasn't going so quietly this time.

'You're just going to watch me get on that plane?'

'You have your job...'

'But you're just going to kiss me half to death then drive me to the airport and wave me off into the sunset?'

He winced. 'I'm not going to enjoy it...'

God, she hoped he was talking about the parting and not the kissing.

'You're not going to ask me to stay. Or even hint?'

'What right do I have to expect that of you? To throw in your career for me?'

Confusion tore at her heart. Because he had *no* such right, but that was exactly what she wanted him to do. Because that meant he wanted her *here*.

When doing nothing meant he didn't.

'So what was this, then?' She flicked a trembling hand in the direction of the sofa. 'A casual bit of sport?'

His eyes skirted across the trees. 'You must have felt the chemistry—'

'Oh, that was you letting off a bit of accumulated steam?'

'*That*,' he barked, and it was mostly mist, 'was me wanting to answer a question that's been five years in the making.'

To be fair, she'd had that exact same question… But she wasn't feeling all that fair right now. Not when the first thing out of his mouth after leaving hers was a reminder of her departure. As if he didn't want her to forget.

Or maybe assume.

'And did you get your answer?' she whispered.

'Yeah,' he breathed, his face perplexed. 'I did. But like all important questions, answering it has only raised more.'

She snatched up the quilt and dragged it around her shoulders. No point both of them suffering from exposure. 'Like what?'

'Like why you kissed me back with such enthusiasm if it was such a bad idea.'

How about because she had zero self-control around him? Or because out here in the forest she'd imagined for a moment that real-world rules didn't apply. The rules that said sensible women didn't kiss men they knew they'd never see again.

'I leave in *hours*, Will. What is the point of starting something we can't finish?'

So much easier to say—to think—now that they'd stopped.

'Something tells me we are well and truly finished now,' he muttered.

The sarcasm did exactly what it was supposed to do—it forced distance between them. She recognised the protective mechanism even as she went with it. She edged towards the front of the deck and away from him as he spoke.

'You have a life to go back to, tomorrow—'

'Not much of one.'

'—a career.'

'That I'm not exactly loving.' She was too angry to be reasonable.

Will threw his hands in the air. 'Your being dissatisfied with your life is no reason to assume you can just move into mine.'

Kitty reared back as if the blow had been physical, and time collapsed around her.

The years since he'd last accused her of insinuating herself into his world dissolved into nothing. She tried to speak but the word came out more of a pained croak.

Will hissed.

'What I mean is...' He grasped around for a better way to say what he obviously wanted to say. But he didn't find it. 'No, I guess that's exactly what I meant. I'm not a ticket out of your imperfect world, Kitty. You're going to have to sort that for yourself.'

Her chest heaved beneath the quilt as much as Will's did beneath his coat. *Her* coat, the one she'd borrowed from him so many times.

That little intimacy nearly broke her.

'I guess there's nothing left to say, then,' she finally said, controlling her speech as tightly as she clutched the quilt.

He took a moment to gather himself, and he stood, back to her, while she was powerless to do anything but stare.

What could you say when you'd just had your heart ripped out?

Again.

'I've got a job on in the morning,' he said, turning back briefly. 'Not sure if I'll be home in time for the airport run. You'd better plan an extra thirty minutes for the taxi.'

The rising grief had finally subsumed her vocal cords, preventing her from answering. She could only nod.

'Good seeing you again, Kitty.'

And then he was gone. Only feet away but somehow already across the world. He would be gone in the morning—he'd be sure to be—which meant the rigid set of Will's back and the judgement bleeding from his eyes like the green from the aurora would be her final memory of him.

Her fingers drifted up to her lips.

When she wasn't dreaming of that kiss.

She sank back down onto the sofa and stared up into the blazing light show. Had she imagined it dancing before? Now, it seemed to shift more like the mourners behind a funeral procession, peering down on her in silent concern and compassion.

And not a small amount of bewilderment.

CHAPTER TWELVE

'I TRUST THE TOWN took good care of you,' the taxi driver checked, setting her wheeled luggage on the airport kerb. 'Next time we see you I hope it will be under less dramatic circumstances.'

He meant the emergency landing, but it applied just as well to the scene out on the deck last night with Will.

But, no, a return visit was definitely not on the cards.

'Thank you.'

Will had been as good as his word, making himself—and his dogs, as she'd sadly discovered—completely absent while she readied herself to leave. She'd had a twenty-minute wait for one of the two taxis in town and she'd passed it at Will's dining table, sitting stiffly, dreading—but breathlessly waiting—for him to walk back in. So that she could apologise. So that she could say goodbye.

So that they could get some closure.

In the end a hastily scribbled note had to suffice for all three. Will probably covered off on his last night.

'Welcome back, Ms Callaghan. We so appreciate your patience...'

The woman at the check-in counter was in full service recovery mode, and readied herself for the barrage of complaints she'd obviously had from other delayed passengers. But Kitty was in no mood to fight for justice.

She was in no mood for anything that took energy.

'No problem,' she muttered, peering out of the massive wall of windows.

Sure enough two small aircraft sat there, modern jet engines, but designed for no more than thirty people. She'd certainly travelled on much worse, but the sight of them sitting out there as slick as the film of ice on the tarmac left her feeling more dismal than usual.

In an hour, she'd be in the air, leaving Churchill behind her. An hour after that she'd be back in her hotel room, juggling room service and her overdue edit. The morning after that, she would be on her way back to Los Angeles and an apartment in dire need of a good airing out.

Boarding pass in hand, she turned and wandered towards one of a dozen empty seats in the small terminal.

'You don't understand…' a tense young woman was saying at the adjacent desk. 'I need to get to Winnipeg as fast as possible. My sister's in early labour. I'm her birth buddy.'

She wanted to tell the stranger that, yeah, they did understand, and empathise, but there was just so little they could do about the numbers they were trying to ship out on such a limited number of seats. She wanted to tell her that—six days ago—she would have been just as frustrated, but that spending time in Churchill had a way of changing how you approached life. She felt no urgency, now, although CNTV were screaming for her edited story and she knew she needed to get far away from Will. Inside her head, it was all very calm.

The hour would pass, the plane would depart, life would return to normal.

Although she wasn't sure she ever would.

'Your flight leaves right after the first one,' the woman assured the panicking passenger.

'The flight I'm on zigzags through every mining, milling and hydro town between here and Winnipeg,' the woman cried as Kitty sank into one of the wide plastic chairs. 'It's going to take hours. There must be something you can do for me?'

One day ago, Kitty would have happily given up her direct plane seat for this woman.

How much difference a day made.

Sorrow blanketed her heart, cold and heavy. She didn't have the energy to pull out her tablet and get stuck into her share of the complimentary Wi-Fi. Or her laptop to continue editing the Zurich story. Or her diary to see what the next few weeks held. She did have enough energy, though, to stare sadly at the massive polar-bear skin hanging in the display case on the wall across the terminal and feel a certain amount of empathy for it.

She felt just as flat.

Laid just as bare.

Fool me once, shame on you. Fool me twice...

Who was she kidding, imagining for a moment that there might be a happy ever after for her and Will in his fairy-tale forest? Or thinking that she'd miraculously earned some kind of second chance. She'd walked squarely into last night and had no one to blame but herself. Five years ago, he'd let her infatuation run until it had got uncomfortable enough to call a halt to. Maybe it had been mutual to start with, maybe it had just flattered him or amused him; regardless, he'd pulled the pin on it on his terms, not hers.

Last night he'd gone one better and kissed her—repeatedly—fully intent on still putting her on her plane today.

That was not cool.

That was not the man she thought she knew.

How was she supposed to put Will out of her head, now? Her heart? Knowing how well he kissed, how good he tasted, how comfortably her body fitted into his on that sofa. Hard enough doing it after Nepal when she hadn't ever touched him, but now…

Ugh.

And how was she supposed to go back to work for CNTV—all its fierce rivalry and treachery—knowing, now, that she would have said yes in half a heartbeat if Will had asked her to stay. As clear as the air in Churchill—she would have embraced a new and simpler life and she would have done it with wide-thrust arms.

She couldn't just turn off that kind of discovery.

Everything she'd worked for, everything she'd sacrificed at the demanding altar of success meant absolutely nothing against the possibility of a future with Will Margrave, and it was *because* she had such ambition that she wanted more. She wanted it all. The man. The family. The creatively satisfying career.

The life.

That was where her ambition lay now.

Maybe she'd never been cut out for the fast track at all. Just like Marcella, maybe she'd put so much of herself into creating a new persona she couldn't bring herself to walk away from it.

One thing was crystal clear… If she was going to sacrifice all the things she wanted most, it was not going to be for some mid-level correspondent role in the gladiator arena of corporate news. If she had to be alone then she wanted to be creating her stories on her timeline, her way. Like the hobo she was at heart.

Hadn't she earned that?

As the freedom settled like fresh snow on her mind, a weight as colossal as the A340 that had brought her to Churchill lifted off her and fell away, like the lid of a coffin that she hadn't even realised she was imprisoned in. A coffin made of glass—she could see out but nothing could get in. No hope. No happiness.

No air.

Kitty shot to her feet, stumbled to the exit and practically fell on the button for the power doors. They whooshed open and pure, oxygen-saturated, throat-hurting air rushed in and shocked her awake from a sleep half a decade long.

She couldn't go back.

She couldn't stay, either, not here, but she just couldn't—she *wouldn't*—go back to her job or her stuffy little apartment in Los Angeles or her single-focus life the way it was. Will's latest rejection didn't hurt any less for being awake again—if anything it hurt more—but his rejection had led her to this realisation; his kisses had woken her from her coma. But his rejection had also brought her back full circle, to the place and person she was when he first sent her away and, for that, she would always be grateful to him. And she would always miss him.

And mourn him for ever.

At the counter, the woman kept on arguing.

Out on the tarmac, her flight kept on refuelling.

Standing half in and half out of the terminal door, Kitty kept on breathing.

Will rested his forehead on the timber top of his dining-room table, the note clenched in his fist, refusing to look at the clock over his kitchen. If he didn't know the time, then he didn't know whether or not Kitty was still in his town or whether she was a kilometre over Manitoba. Whether he still had time to catch her or whether her plane was accelerating down the runway even now. Whether she was gone from his life as he'd accepted or whether she might still be in it for just a few minutes longer.

He'd run the dogs hard this morning—too hard judging by their sideways glances and gun-shy expressions on returning—because speed was the only thing that kept him from imploding. The sharp sting of snow on his face. The numb ache of the cold. If he couldn't feel his skin then maybe if he just kept going he'd stop feeling his other organs, too. One by one, until that lump in his chest stopped aching for good.

He couldn't take her to the airport. He knew he didn't have it in him to stand politely waving as Kitty taxied away from him.

Not again.

If that made him a coward, so be it.

He turned his head sideways and loosened his fist on the paper.

Dear Will,
Thank you for the refuge. My unscheduled
stay in the north was both enlightening and
exhilarating...

Her choice of language plucked at the fibres deep in his chest. Not 'thanks for the bed' or 'appreciate the hospitality' or 'cheers for the accommodation'. Subconscious or not, Kitty went with *refuge*. As if that was the part of it that she'd valued the most—his protection. A refuge was something you sought when times were tough, when you needed to flee from something. When things just got too hard. Exactly what Churchill was for him when he first came here.

He totally understood the instinct.

And he definitely understood exhilaration. He'd been swamped in it out on his deck last night. Too much, in fact. Maybe so much that he had nowhere else to go from there but down.

I wonder how much more of both it would
have been if I hadn't spent half my time with
you unconscious.

It was impossible not to smile, even through the gut-tightening of the 'with you' part. Of all the things he loved, of all the joys his work brought him, he would gladly trade them all for the chance to rouse Kitty from that cosy slumber every single morning. And right there was the great tragedy between them.

Because he could believe it with his head…but not with his heart.

You have yourself a piece of heaven here in the forest, Will, I hope you know that.

Funny, when he thought about heaven at all it always came furnished with the happy, crazy love his parents had shared. He never imagined he'd be enjoying it alone.

The way things ended between us is the only thing I would change about the past days. I didn't want that to be the last thing we remembered about each other. I'm sorry.

Not nearly as sorry as he was. And it shamed him even more that she was apologising to him. For what—being strong enough to own her feelings?

That wasn't a weakness.

Kitty xx

Those were the letters that killed him, those two little 'x's. Because he knew what they stood for. And he knew, now, what two of Kitty's little kisses tasted like, and two were never going to be enough. It was a shame grown men didn't cry because this was the moment for it. The moment that her kind and gentle nature leaked through all the protective spikes. She couldn't help making good on what *he'd* caused.

'Idiot,' he murmured into the table timber, rubbing his thumb over Kitty's signature on the note. 'Freaking idiot, Margrave.'

He'd had this exact same conversation with himself five years ago as Kitty's taxi had rattled away down the hill. When he'd sent her away rather than manning up and confronting their attraction. Last night, he'd seen Kitty's hurt—practically tasted it on the frozen air—but he'd still walked away from her without explaining why.

And—once again—Kitty had paid the price for *his* lack of courage.

He simply wasn't up to history repeating itself.

He'd worked his guts out trying to save his marriage over the three years after Kitty had left, trying to be there for Marcella when maybe what he'd really needed to be doing was packing her up and sending her the heck home. Back to the conservative life she'd fled. But he hadn't—because he'd known it would kill her, spiritually, to slink home with her tail between her legs. Or worse, to be sent. And he knew she was too Southern to go back on her commitment to him. And so he'd let it slide, tried to bring her joy in other ways. But he'd failed in that just as, ultimately, he'd failed Marcella.

And then the quakes had done, literally, what he'd been afraid he'd do, spiritually.

Seriously… Someone needed to revoke his search and rescue licence with protective instincts like that.

Churchill was no prize despite its northern charms. It was remote, sometimes hostile, dead quiet except when it was bulging at the seams in tourist season, and services had a habit of simply stopping for random hours on end. That kind of life—that kind of solitude—wasn't for everyone, especially a pathologically busy woman more used to international hobnobbing. Yeah, old Kitty had loved Nepal, but she'd only been there ten days and, just like Pokhara, a few days up here was a far cry from a few months. Or years.

Marcella had loved those first weeks, too.

What if Kitty hated the place—and him—after a few months? Sending her away now was hard enough. What hope that he would ever find the courage to do it after he'd had her in his life? In his bed. In his heart.

Will pressed his thumbs to his throbbing temples.

Who was he kidding? She'd already set up a little base camp in there. She'd been there for years, quietly in her own little corner refusing to be completely set aside, resisting his efforts to wedge her back down. In his heart she was still running up and down the slope in Pokhara, playing with his dogs and embracing the Nepalese and their mountain lifestyle. If she could find genuine joy in a run-down village at the base of the Himalayas, couldn't she lean to love a small town in the sub-arctic?

And shouldn't it be her call?

His head came up.

Who was he really protecting by sending her away? He couldn't kid himself it was his marriage, this time. Or Kitty, given how destroyed she'd looked last night. There was only one person he was protecting by banishing her from his world again.

Five years ago he'd let her leave Nepal believing she was the failure. The least he could do—*the best he could do*—was not send her away from Churchill believing that again.

'Screw it,' he said and looked up at the clock.

Afterwards, Will wondered what might have happened if he hadn't sat at his dining table for quite so long contemplating the semiotic subtext of Kitty's farewell letter. Or if he'd cut ahead of the cab leaving the airport rather than courteously waiting for it to pick its way across the pocked and icy entryway. Or if he'd parked in the tow zone to get inside quicker.

Would any of those things have made the slightest difference?

As it was, he'd stood in the little airport terminal, his palms resting impotently on the icy glass, and stared at the lights of her departing flight. It was barely a glimmer now, through the steady snow, almost at the end of the runway. But it was categorically *gone*. And it had taken Kitty with it.

He got no points at all for a fruitless eleventh-hour airport dash.

Much too little, way too late.

'Did she forget something, Mr Margrave?' a friendly voice said from behind him.

He turned his confusion back to the airport staffer. 'Who?'

'Your billet.' Then at his blank expression she clarified, 'I was the one who called you earlier in the week.'

He shook away his irritation. It wasn't this woman's fault that he was such a monumental screwup. 'No. I was just hoping to catch her before she left. To tell her something I'd…forgotten.'

'You've got about seven minutes, then.'

That brought his gaze up again before it snapped back out to the empty runway. 'What? Didn't the chartered flight just leave?'

'Ms Callaghan swapped tickets with a woman who needed it more. Her new flight has just finished loading up…'

Will followed her finger where she pointed out of a side window. A twenty-four-seater sat there, waiting.

'Scheduled to leave in seven minutes. Oops, six now—'

She didn't get any further, and Churchill just wasn't set up with the right kind of security to stop a steam train from barrelling through the doors out onto open tarmac. Will's sled boots hooked into the icy surface of the asphalt as the door swung shut behind him.

'Mr Margrave…? You can't—'

That was as far as the anxious woman got and the staff on the runway could do little else but look up as a steam train sprinted past them for the fold-down steps. He burst onto the waiting plane in a flurry of displaced snow.

'Will?' Kitty's voice squeaked at him from near the back of the plane. 'What are you doing here?'

A dozen curious eyes stared at him and one very anxious flight attendant telegraphed her alarm in the tense grip on his forearm.

'You haven't left.' The spectacular redundancy of his announcement struck him and he struggled to find a way to make the statement—and the scene he was making—a little less absurd. 'Why not?'

'Someone was desperate to get home fast,' Kitty said, as if that explained everything. 'I gave her my seat on the direct charter.'

The hostess tugged on his arm. 'Sir, I'll have to ask you—'

But he paid her no heed. 'And you're not? Desperate to go, I mean.'

Kitty's eyes rounded. 'I'm...um...'

The flight attendant surrendered her harpy's hold on his arm to turn and alert the captain to his unexpected intrusion in the tiny cabin.

Three minutes. To sum up a lifetime of baggage.

'I got your note,' he said, helplessly, down the aisle, still partly bent over to avoid hitting his head on the low roof. As good a place as any to start.

'Okay...?'

'I wondered if—' Lord, as if this weren't hard enough without an audience '—you might want to talk about it?'

She blinked at him. 'No. I left a note.'

His panic levels rose as the fuel in the jet did. *Right.*

'I just...I wanted to explain myself a bit better. About asking you to leave.'

Kitty's porcelain skin flushed and she glanced around.

It killed him to make a difficult discussion so much harder. Will turned to the flight attendant. 'Look, can we get off for a few minutes...?'

'I wish one of you would.' She glared. 'Security are on their way.'

He knew Airport Security. Justin owed him a few favours, so something told him that he wouldn't be rushing. But this wasn't a quick conversation, either.

Unless he made it one.

'I don't want you to leave, Kitty,' he blurted. 'I want you to stay. With me.'

If her blood thundered any harder it was going to start spurting out of the creases in her skin. Wouldn't that look pretty on this brand-new aircraft?

'You didn't want me to stay. You were very clear.'

He looked as pained as she felt at the memory. 'And now I do.'

'And what if you change your mind again tomorrow?'

'I won't. I've thought it through.'

She took a deep breath. 'So have I. I'm going to make a few changes to my life. And I can't do that here.'

Her words wrapped around her like a shield. She just couldn't take any more hurt today.

'I… Good,' he mumbled. 'If that's what you want. We don't get a second go at life.'

For a few lovely days she'd thought she might have.

'Doesn't it bother you?' he rushed. 'Wondering if you might be walking away from the most amazing thing in your life?'

Yes, it bothered her. But she wasn't about to admit it.

She sat up straighter. 'You have a very robust ego, Will.'

'I'm talking about me, letting you leave.'

The flight attendant glanced at her watch and stepped closer to Will. Any second now Security were going to rip him out of that door like some kind of full-body alien abduction.

'I'm not sure that more time is going to help you answer that.'

'Give me a chance—'

'You've had your chances,' she pressed. 'Two of them. And you blew it both times. I get that you were confused the first time—' *and married* '—but what's your excuse now?'

He wanted to answer; she could see it in the pinch of his face. The fold of his brows.

'You're protecting yourself from something,' she went on. 'But I need someone who will protect *me,* Will. Do you understand?'

The confession came from somewhere dark and cobwebby. Somewhere she'd never really poked around before. She didn't even know that was what she wanted until she heard it in her own voice.

But it was truth.

She wanted someone to put her first. Even if she fought them on it.

Her fellow passengers weren't even trying to be discreet any more. Their faces swivelled between the front and back of the plane like a Wimbledon crowd. Even the attendant forgot her obligations long enough to become engrossed.

'Marcella thought she wanted me but it was the dream she wanted—heroic husband, bohemian lifestyle, exotic country. Really she just wanted out of her family situation. And I was her exit. And then you were so unhappy with your job...'

Last night suddenly made so much more sense.

I'm not a ticket out of your imperfect world...

'You thought I was using you?' she whispered, horrified.

'No, Kitty, I... Not now.'

'But you did? Last night?' The air puffed out of her. 'The second time I gave you my heart wrapped in a big bow and you thought it was... what...some kind of lazy whim?'

'It was a fear, Kitty. It wasn't rational.'

'I'm not Marcella, Will.'

'I know.'

'And I wasn't using you. I just didn't want to lose you again.'

'You don't have to. Stay.'

'No.' Anger made her rash. Tired of being messed around. Even by him. *Especially* by him. 'I'm quitting my job. As soon as I get back. You were right that I need to take control of my own happiness.'

Will's face fell. 'Tell me you haven't had a taster this week. Of what we could be together. *How* we could be.'

Saying it again wasn't going to change anything so she just stayed silent. Her eyes dropped to her lap.

The whole flight looked to her. Wanting an answer to the unanswerable.

She looked back up at him. 'You broke my heart in Nepal, Will. By sending me away. You made me think that my feelings were something dirty. Then you made me feel the same way last night.'

'Kitty, I—'

'And again just now. But they're not, Will. They're the purest and most honest thing you would ever have known.'

She curled her fingers around the clasp of her

seat belt. 'I have a story to finish, a job to quit and an apartment to sublet. Then I'm going home to Sydney to start over. I have so much work ahead of me and none of it is getting done sitting on this tarmac.'

Security arrived at the planeside, drawing Will's attention away.

'You leaving won't stop me from loving you,' he gritted as a security guard stepped up behind him in the doorway and clamped an authoritative hand on his shoulder.

Behind Will, the flight attendant gasped more loudly than Kitty did and it drew most of the passengers' focus off her just as she needed the respite. Just as her world dropped clean away from her as the tundra would be from this plane in about thirty seconds.

'You don't love me,' Kitty choked.

Thud, thud, thud...

'I beg to differ,' he said, all confidence despite the audience. As if just saying the words gave him a shot of courage. 'I've loved you for five years. I just didn't let myself.'

'You barely knew me, then, Will. You don't know me any better now.'

'Easily remedied,' he urged. 'Stay. And let me in.'

But, of course, she couldn't. Not if he could ever think she would use him like that.

'I'm sorry, Will,' she whispered.

It was only then that his eyes dropped to her white-knuckled grip on her seat belt. But he didn't go without a parting comment.

'Promise me that wherever you go next, whatever you end up doing, you'll do it for yourself, because it makes you happy,' he said as the single hand on his shoulder was joined by a second one on his arm. 'Not because anyone else has an expectation of you.'

There were too many tears in her throat to have a prayer of answering him. Besides, the insistent hands were now dragging him out of the plane. But Will used the final seconds before the attendant pulled the steps shut to catch her eye and hold it. Long enough that he saw her nod. It was the easiest—and the hardest—agreement she'd ever made.

The plane door and the one between the cockpit and the cabin were secured. Kitty turned her face to the window to avoid the speculative glances of her fellow passengers—or, worse, the compassion—as the aircraft started backing out into the runway apron, battling the flood of tears that she couldn't release. Not here.

Everything Will had said was pinging around her mind. That he'd been burned by Marcella. That he'd been afraid. That she needed to sort herself out.

That he loved her.

The idea of it was as terrifying as it was revolutionary. No one had loved her before, and she hadn't loved anyone either. Anyone but unattainable Will. Because if you ran hard enough and long enough then people only saw how incredibly busy you were and they failed to notice how lonely you were.

And if you did for enough years...then you did too.

A girl could go her entire life that way.

Sudden sorrow soaked into her like the melting permafrost of the Boreal that she could only just see beyond the snow out of her window. Then a breathless tightness slammed into her just as the aircraft began to taxi towards the runway.

'Are you all right?' the flight attendant asked as she did her final pre-flight check up and down the cabin. 'You're very pale.'

'I'm...um...'

Impossible to speak without air in your lungs, and to describe her body's reaction to leaving Will behind for ever. Even though it was what she wanted.

Apparently, not all of her agreed.

'Perhaps you need some air.' The flight attendant reached over her to operate the nozzle above her seat but then examined her critically. She searched right in behind her eyes. Finally, she clucked, her face full of conspiracy. 'No. That's not going to be nearly enough.'

As soon as Will was off the plane and the aircraft door was sealed, the airport's security, Justin, wordlessly dropped his firm hold on him. They'd flown bear rescues together. Justin knew he wasn't going to cause a scene. Not further than the one he'd already caused, anyway. He led Will a safe distance away and then stood officially by as Kitty's plane squared up on the runway. There were a dozen windows on the aircraft but hers was on the other side so Will wasn't even going to get a final glance. Just…nothing.

Grief sat like a stone in his gut.

He'd failed—again. But at least this time he'd taken a risk. Put her first. And if nothing else, then Kitty was leaving Manitoba knowing that he loved her.

What might that be like—being actually and genuinely loved?

Marcella never had loved him. Not truly. And if Kitty did she would have stayed, wouldn't she?

'Sorry, Will,' Justin said quietly. 'I have to escort you off-site.'

Will kept his gaze firmly pinned to the thickening snow and the tail lights fading within it. 'Yeah, okay.'

He started to turn, but as he did Justin frowned and squinted out into the airfield. 'What the—?'

Kitty.

He knew it, without even turning around. He knew it because his skin prickled and his chest swelled with hope. And because a moment later Justin's radio started to go ballistic.

Will turned in time to see a little reddish figure emerging through the snow, jogging towards the terminal on the slick runway apron. Behind her, the lights in the fog stayed put.

'I am so dead,' Justin muttered.

Kitty slowed her jog fifty feet or so away from Will, but just as he thought he'd catch her eye her left leg went out from under her on the ice and she hit the tarmac with a bone-cracking thud. Without waiting for permission—without even asking for it—he bolted away from Justin and negotiated the slippery asphalt, skidding to a halt next to where Kitty writhed. He scooped down to her and slid his arms under hers and pulled.

She turned her face up to his and said the words he'd been waiting five years for.

'Son-of-a—'

Okay, so it wasn't the words themselves. It was the ones between the lines. Her presence spoke volumes.

He hauled her up.

'Why are you smiling?' she grumped in lieu of thanks. 'I think I just broke my hip.'

Lord, if she cursed at him every day for the rest of his life he'd be absolutely thrilled. 'You're too stubborn to break anything.'

He got her stabilised on her feet but he was in no mood to let her go.

'So that was pretty dramatic,' he said, trying to keep the raw hope from his voice. Trying to keep her close.

She peered up at him. 'I changed my mind.'

'And everyone else's.'

'I'm sure the rest of the flight will be woefully

uneventful by comparison to the show we just put on, but they can take off without me.'

'Not with your luggage on board, they can't. Whole plane will have to be unloaded and re-checked.'

She turned back to those irritated tail lights still sitting out in the snow waiting for instructions from…somewhere.

'Oh.'

He couldn't shake the smile still plastered to his face.

'You broke the law, Kitty.' She didn't deny it. In fact, she looked pretty pleased with herself. 'That's two of us in one day.'

'I wanted to explain something to you… Besides,' she brushed off, 'technically I disembarked on staff orders. Kind of.'

That part of the story could wait.

Will steered Kitty back towards the ice-free safety of the terminal as Justin jogged past them towards the grounded flight. They let the gathering snow give them sanctuary as it swilled around them.

'Let's go,' Will said. 'Before they throw us out.'

CHAPTER THIRTEEN

'Aren't there bears out there?' Kitty asked as Will helped her limp towards a loading door, by-passing the terminal entrance completely.

Déjà vu.

'Bears don't really like the airport.'

'Someone might have mentioned that a week ago.'

It felt like a lifetime ago. Actually, it felt like someone else's lifetime ago. Could a person change that much in six days?

'Through here...'

Will opened a side door, which let them inside the terminal just a few metres from the exit. In moments, they were through and back out into the grey of the car park.

'My bag...'

'Leave it, we'll pick it up later.'

'Can we just cut and run like this? After causing an international incident?'

'You want to go back and explain yourself?'

Good point. How could she, when she barely understood herself?

'Where's your truck?' she puffed, instead.

She thought he'd take her back to his cabin, but they were closer to his land on the edge of Hudson Bay, so Will turned right out of the airport drive and not left. With half the journey already made, it only took ten minutes on quiet white roads to get there. Even the snow lifted a little the closer they got to the bay.

'You want heating or you want to see out?'

If Will put the heater on then the windows were going to mist over within minutes. There was a risk of that anyway, the way her chest was heaving.

'I want to see.'

He killed the engine and tucked his collar higher. Before them, the deep grey silence of Hudson Bay stretched as far as they could see. Stoic, steady, non-demanding. As if it accepted any and all who came to sit there. As if neither of them had to justify today's behaviour to anyone.

'No bears?' Kitty noticed after a moment.

'Maybe there's a dozen of them over in the willow,' he said, glancing at the place the sun would be if it weren't socked in again by cloud. 'Who knows?'

On instinct, she wanted to lock her door—even if bears didn't have prehensile thumbs. This close to the water a little fog hung wispy and pretty against the backdrop of the bay.

'It's so beautiful here. Marcella would have loved to paint it.'

Will stared out at the water. 'She would have.'

'I'm not her,' Kitty said after a moment.

He turned to her. 'I know.'

'But my life *is* hollow,' she acknowledged, her head bowed. That was a more palatable word than 'empty'. 'And that's not a good reason to be with someone.'

His throat lurched. 'Yet, you're here.'

She stared at him and finally—finally—whispered from that place deep down inside where she kept all her secrets. 'What if that's what this is?'

'Is that all you think we are?'

This thing zinging between them. Even now.

'I don't know. I've carried a torch for you for so long. Maybe I just didn't want to feel alone, all this time.'

'Or...' he pressed a kiss to each of her eyes in turn, so gentle and so full of hope it physically hurt '…maybe you were alone all this time simply waiting for me? You just didn't know it.'

Deep inside, something unfurled and reached for the shaft of light his words created. Something that had lain dormant for a very, very long time.

'You don't think I'm using you?'

Will curled his warm fingers around her cold ones.

'Marcella was desperate for a life of her own, a life of beauty, and I thought that would be enough between us, that we could grow a solid marriage on that. But it was as unsteady a foundation as the rock under our hill turned out to be.' Those beautiful blue mirrors creased. 'I didn't want that to happen with us. I was afraid of that.'

There was something about such a strong man admitting his fear… It made it possible for her to say anything.

'I was so jealous of the life you had in Nepal with Marcella,' she said. 'I thought it was perfect. So easy and equal. I would have traded spots with her in a heartbeat. Because she had Nepal and she had the life. And she had you.'

His smile slipped and she knew she'd hurt him a little. Because his life with his wife had not been at all enviable. And he would always carry that on his shoulders.

'Why did you kiss me, Will? Why not just let me fly off in the morning? If that's what you wanted.'

His head dropped. 'I'd been wanting to kiss you since you bought this damned coat.' He ran his fingers up its cherry padding. 'But things were just too...prickly before the dog run.'

'If I was defensive it was only because I was scared.'

'Of what?'

'That I was intruding—again! That I was no more welcome this time than last. And that you might be constantly searching my face for signs of rekindling infatuation. You were the last one I was going to show that to.'

Understanding dawned in his eyes. He pressed back and brushed her hair with both hands, then pressed his palms either side of her face and he just looked at her—for eternity—wanting her to see him. Really see him.

'Infatuation like this, you mean?'

'I don't want to leave,' she blurted. 'I know I should, I know it would be the grown up and responsible thing to do, but I can't leave you behind. Not twice.' She dropped her head to his shoulder.

He tucked her in close. 'You can stay as long as you want, love.'

Love.

'You're like a dog with a new toy with that word.' Making light of it bought Kitty time to grow used to it. It brought it into the realm of everyday.

When it was anything but.

'It's the novelty.' He smiled. 'My uncle was fantastic but he wasn't *parents*, you know? I spent my childhood feeling sure there must be more to love. Thank God for my uncle's dogs…'

Suddenly his career choice came into sharp focus. All that hairy, unconditional love.

'And then Marcella.'

'She was so beautiful and fragile, like some kind of ethereal creature. I was completely smitten. I married her determined that I could *make* her love me back through sheer determination. If I tried hard enough. If I worked hard enough. But then I met you.' He smiled. 'And it was immediate. I finally knew what it looked like, what I was striving for and how easy it should be. But, I wasn't free to have it.'

For the first time, Kitty recognised that she

might not have been the one doing it toughest when she drove off that mountain five years ago.

'You have a lot to answer for, Will Margrave,' she muttered. 'I blamed my career for every relationship that failed to launch, but really it was just that none of them could live up to the standard you set. I couldn't shake you.'

The thought of living a life without him in her heart was almost inconceivable. That was why she'd scrambled off that plane when the flight attendant had given her the out. Not quite as dramatic as the one a week ago, but close.

His smile, then, rivalled the aurora from the night before. 'I like to think I'm memorable.'

Despite the lack of heating, the truck's windows were getting well and truly fogged up now. Robbing them of view but giving them a safe little igloo instead. Will leaned in and pressed his mouth to hers; gently, giving her plenty of scope to protest.

She didn't. Not at all.

'Tell me about quitting,' he said when the kiss ended.

She leaned back. Found his eyes. Considered her answer. 'I took a wrong turn five years ago and I've been charging off in the wrong direction ever since.'

A direction that didn't include Will.

'When did you discover that?'

There was still a note of caution in his voice. But she didn't resent it. Instead, she understood it.

Huh. There was a novelty. *Understanding* Will. Instead of doubting him, instead of fighting him.

'I think I've known for a while. I just hadn't admitted it to myself,' she said softly. 'The last time I was truly happy was in Nepal.'

'Churchill isn't Pokhara,' he warned.

'That's okay, I'm not the same me. I'm not looking to replicate what we had there.' *We...* 'I just want it in spirit. All the freedom. All the beauty.' She turned to him. 'All the love.'

Will stiffened below her cheek and eased her away from him so that he could peer down into her face, his gaze cautious but no less hot. It fairly turned the cold truck cabin into a sauna.

'Are you talking about the Nepalese?'

Their faith and their love for it had certainly been inspiring but, no. 'I'm talking about you. And me.'

'What are you saying?'

She knew what she was saying, but didn't know how to say it. Except by just finding the courage deep inside her. 'I'm saying that I will find beauty and freedom anywhere you are, Will Margrave. I'm saying that maybe I...love you, too.'

It was imperfect but it was a start.

'Maybe?' Will risked before swallowing heavily. 'Or do?'

Something shifted in the ground beneath them. Clunking into place with the kind of relief a glacier might feel when it finally reached the coast. And she knew exactly what to say.

'I do.'

If the windows weren't already so frosted over he would have steamed them well and truly over with the kiss he delivered then; long and lingering and thoroughly exploratory. And utterly full of joy.

The ground lurched again. It took Kitty a moment to realise that it wasn't the ground. Will leaned over and wiped his arm across the frosted window to peer out. A pair of curious, beady eyes surrounded by cream fur peered back in as the bear gave the truck another curious nudge with its forehead. He swore and lurched back from the window, then scrabbled to start the vehicle. The shock sound of the smooth engine turning over was enough to send the curious bear running and then lumbering and finally wandering off away from the truck to rejoin the friends that had emerged from the willow.

Will turned his shocked gaze to hers. 'Maybe he wanted us to quit melting his nicely forming ice.'

Not a chance. They were officially contributing to global warming right here, right now.

'This is us, Kitty. Predators and complicated transport and insane insects in summer.'

'And bears and beluga whales frolicking in your bay and some pretty amazing tundra flowers judging by the brochures at the airport.'

'That's just the surface polish,' he said. 'Remote living is not for everyone.'

Kitty knew the caution in his voice wasn't for her. Another woman he'd cared about had withered away, once. Despite his best efforts.

'Given we're both probably on the airport's no-fly list now, I think the government may have decided for me.'

'I don't want the government to decide,' he said,

all seriousness. 'This has to be your choice, Kitty. You have to want this—and me—for the right reasons.'

Love was the most right of right reasons, wasn't it?

She turned to him. 'If I wanted to go back to Australia? What would you do?'

'Go with you.' His answer didn't even need thought. 'If that's what it takes to be with you. *Is* that what you want?'

She looked around them, at the snow field, at the frozen-over wetlands, at the nothing as far as the eye could see. At the complete and utter freedom. And all the stories waiting to be told.

'I think Churchill is about as disconnected and insular as I can be,' she said. And if there was a town ready to accept someone like that it had to be this one. 'Maybe I could be persuaded to think about a relationship with it.'

'Persuaded? How?'

Had she honestly expected him to laugh? He looked almost nauseous waiting for her answer.

She leaned in close and breathed against his lips. 'Nothing terribly complicated.'

And then she kissed him. Touching his lips like snowfall at first, then leaning more fully into him, then clinging to him like the life-preserver his love was.

'I've always loved you, Will. Don't you dare send me away ever again.'

Ardent heat blazed down on her. 'Don't you dare leave.'

EPILOGUE

'MORNING, KITTY!' THE DENE couple across the street called to her as she kicked her boots free of dirt before climbing a few steps up into the hotel diner to meet Will.

She'd just sorted the big film crew from Norway and sent them off with their guide out beyond the river mouth and she had an hour to kill before she was due to meet with the tourism marketing types wanting to set up wildlife webcams all over the district. She had no idea how Churchill had functioned without a permanent media liaison before but she suspected that the council praised the day eighteen months ago that she'd dropped from the sky. Not that she'd be able to keep the pace up for ever, but while she *could* still do it she was very happy to. To give back to the district that had given her so much. Plus it kept her contacts up within the communities she needed to get her documentaries sold.

And they were one of the greatest joys in her brand-new life—her stories, her way, her pace.

And pace was about to become really significant.

'Morning, beautiful,' the other greatest joy said, planting a kiss onto her head and dropping into the seat across from her. 'How's the cub?'

She slipped one hand over her rapidly rounding belly. 'Busy, today.'

'Takes after its mother,' Will said as their young server arrived with fresh coffee.

'You know you won't be able to put this one in your pocket, right?' she warned him affectionately, rubbing big circles over her bump and enjoying the sigh she imagined she felt from the little person within. 'Starsky might still tolerate that but I'm going to get prickly if you try.'

'Are you kidding? Take a cub from a mother as fierce as you?'

'How was the release?'

'Went just fine. Marcella's Point is proving popular for good bear releases. Right on the edge of the conservation reserve but the chopper can land easily without disturbing the status quo.'

The repeat offenders still went a long, long way from town. Just to be sure.

'I've got some news,' Will said. 'About the Churchill Port redevelopment.'

Kitty's head came up.

'Seems the environmental authorities are going to take an eleventh-hour look at the ice-breaker proposal. Thanks to some recent media attention...'

That might or might not have been the subject of the first short film she'd shot here, right after pulling the pin at CNTV.

Mei had made that choice even easier for her by stealing Kitty's story slot and convincing the programme director that she had missed her deadline. But, she'd managed to find some compassion for her—Mei was like an aging queen in a land where youth and beauty were prized above all else and even sheer deviousness hadn't got her anywhere particularly great. And now she wasn't beautiful any more—inside or out. And she'd missed all her chances in life.

From where Kitty sat—full to bursting with Will's baby, enriched every day by this place and the work she got to do in it, loving life and all the possibilities in their future—Mei was like a cautionary tale.

'So what's the buzz in town?'

She always knew, and he always asked.

'We have a pop goddess in our midst. Literally. One of the world's biggest. She's up here with an entourage and a film crew to snorkel with the belugas. You should see their gear—'

Will didn't even flicker an eyelid.

'You don't care, do you?'

'I care that it's good PR for the whales,' he defended. 'And if she gets herself stranded out in the Boreal, I'll care *very* much.' He leaned over the table and kissed her. 'Until then, there's only one goddess in Churchill as far as I'm concerned.'

Kitty kissed him back, pouring all the desire, admiration and respect she had into the man she loved as she breathed against his lips.

'Right answer.'

* * * * *